MW01241335

THE
DEMON
SLAYER

THE DEMON SLAYER

WILLIAM J. EYER
LAWRENCE E. JERALDS

A&L Enterprises
Ava, IL

The Scripture quotations in this publication are from the King James Version of the Bible.

The Demon Slayer by William J. Eyer
Lawrence E. Jeralds

ISBN: **0-9745359-2-3**
Copyright © 1997 by William J. Eyer
Copyright © 2003 by A&L Enterprises

Cover Art by **Jarrett Eyer**
Edited by **Ann B. Jeralds**

Published by:
A&L Enterprises
1531 Hwy 151
Ava, IL 62907

Printed in the United States of America by
BookMasters, Inc.
All rights reserved under International Copyright Law. Contents and/or cover may not be reproduced in whole or in part in any form without the express written consent of the Publisher.

TABLE OF CONTENTS

DEDICATION and
ACKNOWLEDGEMENT

We, the authors, wish to dedicate this text to the Glory
and gift of **Jesus Christ** our **Lord** and **Saviour**.

....

We wish to thank BookMasters, Inc. for their extra efforts
in helping to make this book a reality.

CHAPTER ONE
THE CONTRACT

In the realm between heaven and hell dwell the angels and the demons. They are constantly at war over human souls, awaiting the Day of Judgment promised by the Lord Jesus Christ. One of these mighty warrior angels broke free and invaded the realm of time and space. He blazed across the star-studded night sky, like a shooting star...

The howl of coyotes traveled on the cool breeze of the desert night, sending an unearthly chill down the spine of every man sitting around the campfire. Each was trying not to show his nervousness as Sharp, whose real name was Gregg Green, was pulled into the firelight and thrown to his knees on the opposite side of the fire from where the gang's president stood. Of the several campfires scattered throughout the Demon Slayer's encampment, this fire warmed the leaders of the gang. Sharp, the gang's accountant broke into a sweat as he awaited the judgment of his leader. At the moment, every eye was on Spike, the gang President. He was standing with his back to the fire, staring out into the desert. Holding a cellular phone to his right ear with his shoulder while his hands, with practiced patience, worked mechanically polishing his pearl handled, chrome plated .45 caliber Colt.

Spike stood six feet-five inches tall, thin but very robust. His brown eyes were set in a handsome face but

1

contained a coldness that struck fear in any man careless enough to search them too deeply. Even though Spike was only thirty years old, his hair had already begun to recede making him look much older. He was wearing his usual outfit of tight fitting jeans, jean jacket, and a T-shirt. His T-shirts alternated between pictures of marijuana plants, Satan, and a variety of foul sayings. Tonight he was wearing his, "weed shirt", as he called it, a white T-shirt with bright green leaves and black letters that read, "Thanks for freeing the weed".

As each man listened, not knowing to whom he was talking, they were amazed at how unconcerned their leader acted. They knew only the most powerful people in the world had his private phone number, yet he seemed to treat them with as much contempt as he did everyone else. The men figured a hit man of Spike's reputation and skill could get away with being contemptuous.

Spike, for his part, was already bored with this conversation. He loathed cowardice, and the man on the other end of the phone sounded like a coward. Spike was about to tell him so and hang up, when the man mentioned the city of Covenant.

"Yeah, I've heard of Covenant, who hasn't after two solid years of news coverage? It's Covenant this and Covenant that; for one, I'm sick of hearing about it. Can you hold on a minute?"

There was a pause.

"I know it's long distance, but I have a little discipline problem to take care of; I'll be back with ya in a minute."

Spike, still holding the phone with his shoulder, turned to face the pale accountant, who was still kneeling on the opposite side of the fire, being held by two very large intimidating men.

Spike handed the phone to Winter, his second in command, and ordered, "Read the charges, quickly!"

Winter read, "He took a thousand dollars from the treasury for his own use and Martha over there"; he nodded in her direction, "says that he sexually molested her six-year-old boy." The color drained from Spike's face as he thought, *"another Brother Keller!"* He'd sworn to rid the world of men like Keller, the man who had sexually abused him, when he was a fourteen-year-old boy, named Jarrett White. His heart had grown progressively colder toward God and man since that day.

With undisguised contempt, Spike spat out, "Sharp! What do you have to say for yourself?"

Sharp's forehead was beading with sweat as he whimpered, "Please sir, I'm just sick in the head and I need help."

"Then you admit that you abused the kid, and stole from me?"

"Have mercy on me, sir, please! I'll change my..."

A hole appeared in Sharp's face between his nose, and left eye, as the 45-caliber bullet entered his head. A split-second later the entire backside of his head exploded, as the bullet made its exit, and whistled by the ear of one of the onlookers. The thunder made by the gunshot caused the men to jump, and scattered the coyotes which had drifted a little too close to the encampment.

Spike gestured with his gun and said, "Bury this garbage deep, I don't want the vultures to get sick eating his rotten flesh."

Spike was in a better mood when he retrieved the

phone from Winter, and continued his conversation with the Chairman of the Committee, as if nothing out of the ordinary had just occurred.

"Hey, you still there?"

"Was that a gun shot I just heard?"

"I'm an assassin, remember? Gunshots are commonplace around me. Now, finish your proposal."

The deep voice on the other end of the line had gained an uneasy stammer as it continued, "I want you to go to Covenant and do what you do best. Bully the townspeople, steal, and make the cops look silly, even dirty. When the time's right I'll have some people for you to purge."

"What people?"

"I'll let you know when the time comes..."

Spike interrupted angrily, "You know I want the targets up front! I need time to plan ahead. It's just too risky otherwise."

The man on the other end dripped contempt of his own, "Look, I don't care what you want. I have to stop President Place's re-election next month, and I have to stop this Joshua White character. I'll take care of them, but you must do what I say, or it will ruin the whole plan. We'll pay you your usual one hundred thousand dollar retainer. In addition, we'll pay you the premium price of one million dollars for each person you successfully eradicate on my orders only, of course! Are you interested or not?"

Spike pictured cutting this man's throat with his boot knife for mentioning his brother, Joshua White.

He answered, "Sure! Why not? Except, I want a two hundred thousand dollar retainer; and I want the first million deposited into my Swiss account, before I leave for Covenant. The retainer you can leave in the usual place, and I'll get it on the way to Covenant. Understand?"

The black-souled man on the other end hung up without another word. Spike was unconcerned; he knew the man would pay. He hit the off button on his cellular phone and handed it back to Winter. Spike's "old lady" handed him a cup of hot coffee, but after taking a sip he spat it out, and threw the remainder of the cup into the woman's face, causing her to scream in agony as the hot liquid instantly blistered her face, neck, and chest.

Spike yelled at her, "I've told you for the last time woman! I do not take sugar in my coffee! *Do you understand that now?*"

The terrified woman nodded her head as she watched Spike toss the cup back to her, and put his hand on the handle of his weapon, which he had re-holstered after shooting the accountant. Tears flowed down the woman's cheeks and onto the desert's cooling sands.

"Good! Good!" Spike smiled at her and continued in a calmer voice, "Then would you please be so kind as to get me another cup, and get it right this time?"

Spike turned to his men, having already forgotten the incident; what he saw was anticipation. They wanted to know about this new job. They'd been between jobs for about two months now; their money was running low, while their tempers were running high. Spike took a deep breath. The cool desert air filled his lungs and helped him to center himself. He looked at his camp with pride. His camp was made up of fifty of the meanest, most wanted men in America. He'd collected them over the last few years, and if he had to execute one now and again, as he had tonight, or even if they got themselves killed, he'd simply replace them with someone just as despicable and just as wanted. Each of the men had their own "Crouch Bucket", motorcycle, while their old ladies drove the motor homes, containing their "families", and all of their earthly possessions. Every woman had to be attached to at least one man, but usually went with whomever she was told. The only exception was, Genulata, the psychic, who traveled with the group as their spiritual guide. Genulata, called Sister Gen, had her own motor home, and lived pretty well to herself. She was the only one allowed to back talk Spike and live, but then she knew things that were helpful to him. She had, of course, been wise enough to give him anything he requested of her, including the sharing of her bed, which no other man dared to even ask. This arrangement suited her just fine.

Sister Gen, now thirty-five years old, had run away from home at the tender age of fourteen, to find her freedom. A carnival was working two towns over from her hometown and Sister Gen befriended the carnie psychic who took her in as an assistant. She worked for the carnie psychic, until she could start her own business, which was where Spike met her. She gave him some advice on a future project, which proved to be wise advice. About a week later he came back to congratulate her on the accuracy of her prediction, and he'd talked her into traveling with the gang; she's been a part of it ever since.

It was toward her motor home that Spike now looked. He had the urge to gain some psychic insight on this new project, and then perhaps spend a warm night next to his psychic mentor. Spike was just about to give his men a brief overview of their new job, and then walk over to Sister Gen's, when a sentry yelled, "In Coming!"

Spike reached into his pocket, pulled out a remote control, and with one push of a button, shut the power generator down. When the generator ground to a halt, the entire camp went dark. Spike had devised this system himself for immediate compliance with blackout rules. "The sudden darkness should confuse the intruder." Spike said to no one in particular.

Men all around him pulled their weapon of choice and took up their assigned positions, forming a large, armed circle around the camp. When he reached the sentry's position, Spike took the star-scope, which uses starlight from the night sky to allow the user to see as if it were daylight, from him and looked in the direction the sentry indicated. The star-scope had proven an effective tool in the camp's defense system. The camp had been set up, as usual, in the most remote spot they could find in the desert. They had clear vision for miles around them and could see anyone approaching their position. Four sentries were posted, one at each point of the compass, and each was armed with a star-scope. This practice had successfully warned them of many intruders and helped them overcome several police raids. Skunk, the sentry, puffed up with pride as Spike said, "Way to watch Skunk! That's a hundred dollar bonus for you."

Winter, who was always at Spike's side, made a note of the bonus. By rewarding his men with bonuses and presents, Spike knew they'd all die to get his favored attention.

Spike's attention at the moment, however, was on the ghostly figure that was approaching them at a very high rate of speed. The white figure rode a bike very similar to Spike's own "Crouch Bucket". He liked his men to ride fast, quiet cycles for those times when they needed to get in quietly and leave quickly. The incoming rider's white bike, white leather jump suit, and white helmet, were ablaze as if made of sparkling pearl, which shone against the blackness of the desert night. The rider was crouched low behind the windshield. His white-gloved hands were in perfect control of the power under him. When the full moon suddenly came out from behind a dark cloud, the glow of pearl turned into the radiance of the sun, as it reflected off the rider's white clothes. Spike had to look away for a moment because of the star-scope's sensitivity to light. When he looked again, however, the glow no longer hurt his eyes. An involuntary chill dripped down Spike's spine as he watched this spectral apparition glide on invisible black tires across the desert floor.

As the eerie specter approached, Spike raised his hand, which told the gang to hold their fire and await his command. This order was silently passed around the defensive circle. Without slowing in the least, the intruder veered to the right and began to encircle the camp. At this close range, Spike could tell that the intruder's taste in bikes was impeccable. He was riding one of the fastest bikes ever made. Spike held his breath in awe, as he watched the 145 horsepower, fully aerodynamic bike soar past his encampment.

Spike thought, *"I've got to have this bike!"*

He'd read all about them, in one cycle magazine or another, and knew that this bike was far superior to his own. This was the bike of a leader.

After the intruder had made a complete circle

around the camp, the stranger aimed his rocket directly at Spike. Spike was amazed at the man's skill, but not being a coward, he stood his ground ready for a challenge. He signaled his men not to interfere.

His men held their collective breath and fire, as they watched the bike speed toward their leader. At the last possible moment, the specter applied the brakes and held the bike perfectly straight as it came to a halt not two inches from Spike's boots. The rider just sat there and revved his engine. After a moment, he shut the bike down and got off.

As well as Spike knew bikes, he knew people even better. He could readily tell that the person standing before him had courage, but to come into this particular camp by himself was either foolhardy, or this stranger knew something that Spike didn't.

"No, just stupid", thought Spike.

The stranger reached up and unsnapped the collar of his jumpsuit, releasing his helmet. As he did so, all the weapons that were aimed at the stranger, could be heard clicking into the cocked position. The stranger ignored them, as he removed his helmet.

For a fleeting moment Spike envisioned removal of the stranger's helmet would expose some alien creature from another planet, but the spell was soon broken, when beneath the helmet was found...only a man. He was a man with a strong, kind face and absolutely no fear. The man stood seven feet tall, had a muscular build, and was surrounded by a radiance that commanded respect. Spike didn't like him, and even felt a little threatened by his presence.

The stranger spoke in a gentle, friendly and

confident voice, "Good evening! I hope you don't mind me dropping in like this, but I wanted to meet you."

He'd addressed this to Spike, ignoring all others present. Spike's men chuckled at the thought of anyone wanting to meet the man who was about to kill him, and steal his bike; they'd all read Spike's intention.

"Spike, stop playing with the stranger", someone yelled into the darkness.

Spike said, "I'm sorry, but I don't do interviews, especially unannounced ones!"

Spike gave the expected signal, and several of his men jumped the stranger from behind.

There was an earsplitting clap of thunder, which echoed across the suddenly, cloudless sky of the desert night. The pack of coyotes, which had been working its way closer to the camp, was again frightened away by the sudden noise. Scorpions covered themselves with sand for protection, while tumble weeds were blown about by the sudden rush of wind that stirred the sands into whirling, twisting sand devils. The men, who'd attacked the white figure, were thrown to the ground, some as far away as twenty feet, and they lay there as if dead. As a matter of fact, as Spike looked around he noticed that except for him, all in the camp were now in the same condition. Spike was forced to stand his ground and watch as the white figure transformed into a translucent, dazzling being who, as he rose from the ground, unfurled his magnificent wings to their full ten-foot span.

He spoke in a thunderous voice, "I am Worl, an angel of the Most High God! I have been sent with a message for you, Jarrett White!"

Spike blinked. No one had called him by that name in years!

"Your brother, Chad White, was murdered by the dark forces of Satan over two years ago. Your other brother, Joshua White, will soon be in grave danger, and in need of your help!"

Spike shook from head to toe with a mixture of fear and rage. Fear of this apparition's power and rage at the wetness that was suddenly traveling down his right leg! Spike thought of all the LSD he'd used in the past and then it dawned on him what was happening.

He thought, *"I'm having a flash back! That's it! This is nothing more than a bad trip!"*

He told the angel, "You're nothing but a shadow from a bad LSD trip!"

The angelic warrior drew his sword, pointed it at Spike, and released a bolt of searing light which knocked Spike off his feet, causing him to land on his back some ten feet away. As he gasped for breath, the angel glided toward him just above the desert floor.

Worl said, "Beware, Jarrett White, that you do not bring the wrath of God upon yourself before your time! You will only have one chance at repentance and conversion before the day of your trial overtakes you. Now listen, and heed my words, for the Lord Jesus Christ issued them, Himself! Even though you work for the enemy at the present time, you are to go to Covenant and once there you are to help your brother Joshua. Search deep within your black heart, Jarrett White, and find that mustard seed of the Holy Spirit that even you could not drive out! I'll leave you with this last warning. Watch out for Tumult, Captain of Satan, himself! He seeks to devour your soul, Jarrett White, and he'll come for you soon!"

Thunder rolled across the sky once more, as the angel soared skyward, and instantly blended with the millions of other twinkling lights that filled the night sky. The force of the angel's departure rendered Jarrett White unconscious.

As Worl flew away, he glanced down at the small army of demons who had begun to peek out from behind their cover of motor homes, boulders, and even the unconscious forms of their human hosts. He could tell that they had indeed heard of Worl, Captain of the Battle of Covenant, and they wisely DID NOT want to tangle with him this evening.

Worl felt good as he flew back toward Covenant, and his booming voice shook the earth as he quoted, "*This know also, that in the last days perilous times shall come. For men shall be lovers of their own selves, covetous, boasters, proud, blasphemers, disobedient to parents, unthankful, unholy, Without natural affection, trucebreakers, false accusers of those that are good, Traitors, heady, highminded, lovers of pleasure more than lovers of God; Having a form of godliness, but denying the power thereof: from such turn away.*"

By the time the last of the Scripture had rolled out of Worl's mouth, the demons had been paralyzed with fear; they knew that he was directing this quote at them. He was reminding them that a new war had begun, and their casualties would be high. Several of the demons left to warn their lord, Satan.

CHAPTER TWO
TUMULT PLANS REVENGE

The screams that escaped from Tumult's mouth caused the already terrified demons and human souls to slink even further into the shadows of Satan's personal torture chamber. They were next in line for Satan's personal attention, and knew they had little chance of avoiding their fate.

Satan wasn't happy with the mighty Captain Tumult, who'd failed him at the Battle of Covenant. The Prince of Darkness was close to demoting him to a few centuries in the tar pits, when there was a knock at the door.

Satan frowned at the disturbance and barked, "What is it, I'm busy!"

The door creaked open, and a small, quivering demon announced, "Sir, I'm sorry to disturb you, but you said that you wanted that report on the Covenant Project just as soon as it arrived?"

Satan stomped impatiently and whispered, dangerously, "Yes, well?"

The demon moved aside and several demons warriors entered dragging the limp form of a scout demon into the chamber; and throwing him down in front of Satan, they stepped back and stood at attention, awaiting further orders. The wounded demon tried to get up, but just didn't have the strength.

Satan reached down, grabbed the demon by the

front of his uniform, pulled him to his feet, and shook him.

He yelled into his face, "Report you fool!"

With every ounce of strength left in him, the demon said, "Sir! Covenant has grown in strength. Humans from around the world are flocking there to hear about God, and to be healed by His power, of the illnesses that we've inflicted upon them! Our forces have been driven back to a five-mile perimeter, which we are **not** allowed to cross! We've lost thousands of our soldiers and the number grows daily..."

Satan released the scout, and as the Prince of Darkness screamed in rage, fire shot from his fingertips and burned a large hole into the chest of the scout, and he popped out of sight, only to reappear in the scorching tar pits for punishment.

Satan then yelled at the other demons, "Report Fools!"

They answered in unison; "Captain Worl has declared war again and has already made contact with Jarrett White, trying to turn him to their side! He's also making plans to reverse all of the hard work we've done over the last few years in the United States! He..."

As Satan erupted into another fit of rage, the dodging, scurrying, demons got out of the chamber with only minor burns to various parts of their bodies. The small demon who'd been holding the door open all this time, ducked as a stray lightening bolt hit just inches above his head. He quickly left the chamber, slamming the door behind him.

Satan turned back to Tumult, looking hard and long at his six-foot tall, muscular captain, who'd served him so long and faithfully. Presently, Tumult was tied, spread-eagle fashion, on Satan's personal torture block. Satan looked at Tumult's bleeding feet, where he'd just moments ago, ripped the little toes from of each large foot. Satan looked at the shriveled areas on Tumult's arms and legs, where he'd pulled out one nerve after another, just for the pleasure of hearing this mighty warrior scream like a cadet. Tumult's eyes were black and blue, and were swelling shut from the beatings he'd received. He was gasping to force air into his battered lungs, causing pain as the air passed into the bloody, gaping holes in his mouth, which used to proudly house large, sharp fangs.

After another moment of consideration, Satan walked over to the tortured form of the once mighty Tumult, reached down and gently took his left ear between his thumb and forefinger, and with a sudden, violent jerk, ripped it from his head. Tumult's screams echoed through the chamber, as Satan put the, once useful, ear into his mouth and chewed on it with pleasure.

With his mouth not quite empty, Satan said, "Tumult! I'm going to give you another chance, but I warn you, do not fail me again! You'll go back to earth and crush this new threat. I'm giving you my full authority, and every demon will submit to your orders, just as you must submit to mine. Do you accept my offer?"

Tumult, not being a complete fool, nodded his head as best he could through the pain.

Satan smiled and untied him. Satan then put Tumult's arm around his neck, and gently helped him stand. As an afterthought, Satan healed Tumult's little toes, his fangs, and took enough swelling out of his eyes so

15

he could see again. He also stopped the bleeding from Tumult's left ear cavity, but didn't return the ear. Satan told him that he could have his ear back when he finished the job at hand.

Satan said, as they stumbled toward the door, "You'll report directly to me, Tumult; and I want to be involved every step of the way on this one. Understand?"

Tumult's weak voice answered, "Yes, Master."

As they reached the door, Satan stopped and leaned Tumult up against the wall. He then picked up Tumult's sword that Satan had thrown against the wall in his first fit of rage over Tumult's failure. The blade hadn't broken, but the rubies, diamonds, and emeralds embedded in the hilt of the sword had all popped out, and were scattered all over the floor of the chamber. Satan took the blood red ruby out of his own ring and lodged it in the end of the sword's hilt. This symbol of Satan's authority would give Tumult all the assistance he'd need to accomplish his task.

As Satan handed the sword back to the shaking and weak Tumult, the Dark Lord thundered, in his most authoritative voice, "I want this place cleaned up and ready for my use upon my return!"

Satan then helped Tumult walk out of the chamber, slamming the heavy metal door after them. The poor tortured souls of Theodore Connelly, and Governor Bradley sighed in relief at the departure of Satan and his second in command. Before the echo of either the slamming door, or Satan's final order could fade out, the human souls had already begun the task of cleaning up after their Master's cruel and heartless work. They worked under the watchful eye of the once mighty warrior, Cono, who'd now been reduced to a chamber boss. The scars on Cono's body served to remind him of his own time under Satan's tortuous attentions. Cono cracked his whip on the backs of the two damned souls, and they worked all the faster to please their master.

*   *   *

Spike tried to sit up, but his pounding headache caused him to lie back down again. The blinding desert sun was burning down on him as it rose above the distant foothills. There was a rustling sound next to Spike's right ear, he turned in that direction and tentatively opened his eyelids a crack, and he saw a scorpion scurrying toward him with its tail raised, ready to strike. Spike jumped to his feet, and stomped the scorpion to death, more out of rage than fear.

Memories of last night's "bad trip" came flooding back to him, he was about to laugh it off, when he turned around and his blood ran cold. He stood there, staring at the white motorcycle that sat exactly where the angel had left it. It reflected the morning sunlight, giving the impression it produced it's own light from within. It was beautiful, and Spike ran his hand over its surprisingly cool metal. Spike looked around, for the first time since he'd awakened, and saw that his men were still sprawled all around him, unconscious. Some of the women were peeking out of their homes.

Spike yelled at them, "Make some coffee! Make breakfast! I'll be back soon!"

Some of the women jumped to comply with his order, while others tended to their men, who were just coming out of their forced sleep. Spike jumped on the bike and fired it up. He held in the clutch, throttled back, and then popped the clutch, causing the back tire to spin wildly, throwing sand, rock, and debris all over the nearest men.

They yelled in protest, "Haaay! Watch it Spike!"

Spike quickly reached speeds in excess of a hundred miles per hour, controlling the bike with only his right hand, he put his sunglasses on with his left. The wind blew his hair straight back; it felt good! Spike was determined to clear his head of last night's experience, and to conquer this motorcycle. He'd accomplish the latter, but the experience was forever ingrained in his soul!

*   *   *

Tumult was a hungry demon on the prowl for power, position, and revenge. He raced toward Covenant at an immeasurably fast pace, with his mind soaring as quickly as his body. He was very glad to be free of Satan's wrath, but he had doubts about his mission. Tumult had been beaten twice now by Capt. Worl, the angel in charge of the Battle of Covenant, he wasn't looking forward to facing him again. The throbbing pain on the left side of his head reminded him of the alternative, however, and he quickly brought his mind back to the task at hand.

Just then Covenant came into view, and Tumult came to a screeching halt about seven miles out of town. He wanted to scream in rage, but that would attract unwanted attention, so he ground his new teeth together, and shook in silent rage instead. As far as he could see, in all directions, humans were driving or walking toward Covenant. Over one hundred thousand angels flew between these fools and their God. The sentry had been correct. The area had been totally sealed off from demons. Tumult watched as the demons riding on their human hosts tried to hold on past the designated area. They were attacked by angels who, in very brief but very violent scuffles, caused the familiar and inevitable puff of red smoke that always accompanied the death of a demon. Of course, neither the angels, nor the demons really died in these battles. They simply left this reality and landed at the feet of their masters for judgment. The demons were normally tortured and demoted, to start all over in the ranks, while the angels were healed, praised, and given the choice of returning to battle or undertaking a new task.

As Tumult watched the fierce battle below, he thought of the hatred he had for the soul of Theodore Connelly, the man who used to own the estate grounds to which the pilgrims were now flocking. Theodore Connelly, who was once a Magister IV and Master of the Temple in the local Witch's Coven of Covenant, had made his fortune selling illegal drugs, and had been worth billions of dollars when he so stupidly got himself killed by the enemy. His vast estate, and his billions, had been confiscated by the City of Covenant, and were now being used to build and operate Jesus Park. Tumult had spent a lot of time and effort in the damning of Connelly's soul, and this money, Satan's money, had been accumulated for the purpose of condemning Christianity. Now it supported Jesus Park and promoted Christianity, which was growing daily as pilgrims flocked to worship their

God, and be healed by this bleeding heart, Joshua White.

Tumult snarled, barring his yellowish teeth, as he watched Sam and Barb Crawford pass the five-mile marker. Their demons fought fiercely to stay in control, but finally fell to the overwhelming force of the Angels blocking their way. In the few minutes that Tumult had watched this war, he'd lost over three hundred thousand demons, and was forced to watch as several thousand human souls moved beyond his control.

Tumult swore an oath to himself right on the spot, "I'll personally see to the slow and painful death of Joshua White!" His mood improved as he flashed away from Covenant, and raced toward the damned soul of Theodore Connelly. He'd take some of this loss out of the rancid hide of Connelly, and then he'd get to work on reversing this mockery of justice.

CHAPTER THREE
THE CRAWFORDS MEET JOSHUA WHITE

Traffic was heavy and moving very slowly on the highway leading into Covenant. Sam Crawford's car was threatening to overheat, as was his temper. His car was only three years old; the odometer already read over one hundred thousand abusive miles and it was beyond Sam's ability to pay for repairs. Sam had been an ironworker until about six months ago -- his boss fired him after many months of covering up for his deficient work performance due to alcoholism.

His wife, Barb, was leaning against the passenger door catching a fitful nap. Their five-year-old daughter, Sara, was stretched out in the back snoozing softly. Sam was thankful that the weather had cooled off a bit or it would've been oppressively hot in the car. The fumes, from the other cars, pouring in through the open windows, were bad enough without suffering from the heat. He couldn't take the chance of running the air-conditioner; this would only speed up the overheating of his car's engine.

Life had been weighing heavily on Sam's shoulders for some time and he'd even considered suicide, but that seemed the coward's way out. Sam was an alcoholic but he wasn't a coward. The traffic stopped completely for a moment and Sam took the opportunity to wipe his bloodshot eyes with the sleeve of his denim work shirt. He looked over at his wife's left eye still showing the bruise he'd caused when Barb found out about his gambling debt and made the mistake of confronting him while he was drunk. After he'd sobered up he vowed, for the hundredth time, never to hit her again and he really meant it for the hundredth time! Lurking deep in Sam's soul, however, was the fear that he'd give in, yet again, to the demons of the bottle or the Blackjack table. Both vices were driving him, inextricably, toward despair.

It was his gambling debt, which had first brought that evil man, Starvas Creen, into his life. He'd found out, somehow, that Sam was taking his family to Covenant and Creen approached him just last night, before they left. Creen handed Sam a plastic one-shot gun and told him to kill Rev. Jonathon Smith. He'd given Sam a picture of the man and said that he managed Jesus Park.

Creen had then said, with far too much joy to be bluffing, "You kill him, Crawford, and your debt is forgiven. You fail to kill him, and your daughter dies, whether they heal her or not!" He had then slapped Sam on the back, laughing an evil laugh, as he walked away.

Sam came back to the present when an impatient sounding horn blared behind him. He reached over and lovingly brushed Barb's face with the back of his forefinger and whispered, "I really do love you, honey." As he inched forward in traffic he prayed, "Please help me if you're really there, Jesus! I know I don't deserve your help, but my wife and child deserve better than they're getting! Please don't take your anger out on them; I'm the guilty one! Punish me!"

Just then, something under the hood of Sam's car exploded. Steam shot out from under the hood, the red engine light came on and stayed on.

Sam yelled, "Not my car, Jesus! Me! Punish me!" He shook his fist at the ceiling of his car, and yelled a few nasty expletives.

Barb jumped up and yelled, "What happened Sam?!"

"I prayed to your God, and he zapped my car, that's what! It did me a lot of good to pray..."

"Sam!" Barb exclaimed, "I'm sure God didn't attack you for praying to him, now calm down!"

Sam reared back and almost back-handed Barb, but stopped when he saw the fear in her eyes as she raised her arm her body pressing hard against her door.

Sam put his hands back on the steering wheel, hung his head in shame, and sat there, a beaten man. Barb wept for her husband and his alcoholism, and for her daughter, Sara, who was dying of a cancerous brain tumor.

Sara sat up and wiped sleep from her eyes as she asked, "Are we there yet?" Sara noticed Barb's tears and she asked, "What's wrong Mommy? Why are you crying?"

Sara looked accusingly at the back of her father's head, and that's when she noticed his slumped and shaking shoulders. She knelt behind him, and gave him a hug, as she whispered into his right ear, "It's all right Daddy; we'll find help at Jesus Park." Sara remembered what her mommy had told her about the beatings they both received from time to time, "Your daddy is sick. He has an illness, that makes him drink all the time, and the alcohol makes him do things that he doesn't mean to do.

We'll just try to stay away from him when he's drinking, OK?" A touch of guilt penetrated Sara's heart as she remembered how she'd gotten her mommy and daddy to bring her to Jesus Park. One afternoon, while she was waiting for a treatment at the hospital, she'd seen a program on television about Jesus Park, and a man named Joshua White. He'd looked so kind and friendly that Sara just knew he could help! He was also the last piece to the puzzle of how to help. Sara had heard her parents talking about how the doctors hadn't been able to help her brain tumor. She'd already taken all the treatments, but she still felt very weak and sick. So Sara had decided to tell her parents about Joshua White, and the healings that were taking place at Jesus Park. She'd then proceeded to nag them, ceaselessly, to take her there.

Sara wiped a tear from her eye, as she thought about her parents lack of money; the danger of driving a derelict car over nine-hundred miles; all of the problems they had along the way; and the stress she saw reflected in their faces. Sara reasoned that it was for their own good, and she knew that Jesus would help them, just as He'd helped them to arrive safely at Jesus Park.

Rev. Smith had been walking along the highway away from Jesus Park for quite awhile now.

"I must be nuts!" he thought, for the tenth time, as he wiped the sweat from his brow.

He'd been praying in his own private tent, when the Holy Spirit had prompted him to take a walk out into the line of cars moving ever so slowly toward Jesus Park. He'd learned long ago to trust these little "gut feelings" that he got as he prayed; however, he was beginning to have his doubts about this one. He heard the loud, hissing explosion of a car's radiator blowing a hose. As he walked toward the car, he saw the man as he moved to backhand the woman in the passenger seat. He saw the woman's fear and the man's totally defeated posture, as he slumped behind the wheel of his car. Finally, Rev. Smith saw the little girl as she appeared from behind the man and hugged his neck. As she embraced her daddy, Rev. Smith saw that the little girl had no hair, not even eyebrows. Her bald scalp showed the drawings that the doctors had used to identify the effected area of her brain. Rev. Smith wiped his tears as they mingled with the sweat on his cheeks.

He whispered, "Now I know why you sent me here, Lord. Thank you!"

*　　*　　*

A handsome black man came running up to them, and smiled as he said, "Having some trouble brother?"

Sam yelled, "This old car just can't go another mile, and we don't have any money left to fix it! We're on a desperate journey to see this Joshua White character, to have him cure our daughter of her cancer. Personally, I have my doubts, but as I said, we're desperate!" Sam looked closer at the man and his stomach knotted up, as he recognized the face captured on the picture, which was hidden in his shirt, along with his strange gun.

Sam took a deep breath and let it out slowly. He didn't know why he'd said all of that, especially to the black man he was about to kill, but it felt good to get it out!

25

Sam expected this stranger to yell, or turn away, or something, but instead he whistled and said, "You do have your hands full, don't you! Well, your worries are over now! You've come to the right place! I've seen people come weighted down with troubles, but they always leave light as a feather!

"I can see you're skeptical sir. Well, don't worry! We'll take it one step at a time. For now, just pull off the road over there." As he said this, the man pointed to a small clearing in the curb, which allowed Sam to pull off the road.

As Sam complied with the request, he thought, *"You may solve all my problems mister, but not in the way you think!"*

Sam looked up, and noticed that the man held a radio mike to his mouth, talking to someone. *"What if he was calling security?"* Sam thought as he turned the car off and got out. When he approached the man, he noticed for the first time that he was rather short, about five-feet five-inches, was built rather heavy, his black curly hair was short and peppered with gray. The man's white shirt was wet with perspiration that started under his arms traveled down each side with a third wet streak trailing down his back. The man was fairly beaming with good cheer; Sam had the fleeting thought that maybe this was what Santa Claus does in the off-season.

"Yeah," Sam thought bitterly, *"A black Santa Claus, that's all we need!"*

Sam shook his head as he heard the man say, "That's right, a tow truck and a tram! Thank you, see you then Charlie."

Sam protested, "Look, I appreciate the help, but

26

like I said, I've no money left! How many times are you going to make me say it?! We'll just walk from here, and you can have the junk car."

The man ignored Sam's outburst, and held out his hand, "Look, my name's Rev. Jonathon Smith. I'm the humble manager of these Estates; which we affectionately call Jesus Park."

Sam reluctantly took the offered hand -- he'd always had a problem with black people and wasn't sure he wanted to touch one, especially this one!

He received a very firm handshake, while Rev. Smith continued, "Once you're our guest, you don't pay for anything your entire stay. You have enough to pay for in life; therefore, we give you a small break while you're here. No strings attached Mr..."

Sam said into the silence that followed, "Oh! I'm sorry! My name's Sam, Sam Crawford, and this is my wife, Barb, and my daughter, Sara." He gestured toward the two who'd also gotten out of the car and walked up while the two men were talking.

Rev. Smith smiled at Barb, whom he'd noticed was quite attractive. She was about five-feet nine-inches tall, slim, with short brown hair and brown eyes, one of which had been blackened recently. Rev. Smith took and kissed Barb's extended hand, then knelt down to give Sara a hug.

Rev. Smith didn't miss the barely contained jealousy, or perhaps even hatred Mr. Crawford exhibited. As he picked up Sara, he took a moment to look at Mr. Crawford's six-foot, very muscular frame, despite his out of place beer belly. He also observed the bloodshot eyes, the red nose, the wind burned skin that spoke of an outdoor person, as well as, someone who has abused alcohol for too long! The only thing that was neat about Mr. Crawford was his long, black, shoulder length hair, which was tied back in a ponytail.

His appearance and posture spoke volumes, through which Rev. Smith read about the alcoholism, the prejudice, and even the feeling of being a total failure that was crushing Mr. Crawford. It was Mr. Crawford's defeated and bitter demeanor, which helped the Pastor overlook his prejudiced posture and attitude.

As he stood up with Sara in his arms, Rev. Smith said, "Sam, if you and Barb want to get your bags, we can start walking toward the Park. There's a tram on the way to give us a ride and workers will take your car into town for whatever repairs it needs." Sam began to protest, but Rev. Smith held up his hand and said, "No charge, remember?"

Barb questioned, "No charge?"

Rev. Smith laughed, "Yes, I explained to Sam before you walked over that you pay for nothing during your stay at Jesus Park!"

Barb looked skeptical, so Rev. Smith continued as they walked toward Jesus Park.

"There are twenty square miles of estate here at Jesus Park. It used to belong to an evil man named Theodore Connelly. He was a drug lord and the warlock of the local witch's coven! Through drug sales and extortion, he amassed a fortune worth billions of dollars. During the Battle of Covenant, Mr. Connelly was killed and shortly thereafter the Federal, State, and local governments confiscated his estate, including his billions! The estate was then divided with the local government of

Covenant receiving all of the land of the estate, as well as, two billion dollars of liquid assets! The City Fathers split one billion with the county government; they set up a trust, with the other billion, and appointed a committee to oversee the trust. The sole purpose of the trust is to build and operate Jesus Park, and bring relief to the pilgrims who come here! It's this money that pays for everyone's needs and for the new construction that you'll see as we enter the park! I don't know if you realize just how much a billion dollars is, but believe me, we have quite enough to help you!"

They were approaching a little wooden shack, which was set up on skids. It was to this shack that Rev. Smith now turned his attention.

"Anyone want a nice, cold, glass of lemonade?"

Sara squealed, "Yes! Oh, yes please!"

Then, turning to Barb, she asked, "Can I Mommy? Please!" Barb smiled, "Well yes, certainly! That sounds just heavenly!"

Rev. Smith ordered four lemonades then paid Mr. Jenkins, over his many protests.

As they sipped on their very cold, sweet and sour drinks, Rev. Smith explained, "Mr. Jenkins is allowed to sell his lemonade here to help the pilgrims who have to wait along the road for their turn to enter Jesus Park, it supplements his retirement income as well!"

Sara, who'd just gulped the last of her drink asked, "Do you know Mr. Joshua White?"

Rev. Smith picked her up again, and said, "Why, yes I do, honey, why do you ask?"

Sara smiled, "Because he's going to make my daddy well, and we'll be very happy again!"

Sam choked on a mouthful of lemonade, and finally had to spit it out.

Before he could say anything, Rev. Smith said, "Here's the tram! Sam, if you'll put the bags in the back, we can ride the rest of the way."

A young man of about eighteen was driving, and Rev. Smith introduced him as Charlie Hinkle. Charlie was a tall and lanky youth, with lots of energy to burn, and Sara sat by him in the front seat while the three adults sat in the back. As they bumped along the edge of the roadway, they enjoyed the breeze that their moving vehicle produced. They were shielded from the sun by a cloth top over the tram's frame that also helped to keep them cool. They were all much happier to be riding in the comfort of the tram than to be walking in the heat!

As they cleared the stand of trees, through which they'd just passed, Sam was the first to notice the construction site. There were foundations for three very large buildings. "What're those going to be?!", he asked, more excitedly than he'd intended.

Rev. Smith answered, "Those are going to be three very tall apartment complexes, I believe I was told they could reach as high as thirty stories!"

Sam whistled, and said, rather sadly, "I used to work on buildings like that. I'm a laid off iron worker, you see."

"Maybe you can give us a hand with these babies someday, Sam, but for now I want to help you get settled-in."

As they came up over a little rise, Rev. Smith had Charlie stop the tram and they all got out. Rev. Smith pointed out that the estate was equipped with its own eighteen-hole golf course, tennis courts, swimming pool, and a mansion that was used as an administration building and school for the children. The mansion could be seen in the distance and it looked magnificent! It was located on top of a distant hill surrounded by acres of plush green grass speckled with majestic old oak, pine, and blue spruce trees.

Between the ridge from which they were about to descend, and the ridge on which the mansion stood in its ancient glory, lay a valley that was filled to capacity with what could only be called a tent city. There were row upon row of large tents separated only by small gravel roads. At the end of the tent city, furthest from where the Crawfords stood by the tram gaping, was a large fenced-in field in the middle of which stood the largest tent the Crawfords had ever seen.

Rev. Smith smiled at their reaction, and said, "It's beautiful isn't it? These tents will, of course, be replaced or at least supplemented, by those three apartment buildings that I showed you earlier. That large tent in the middle is our chapel, and if you strain your eyes and look about a quarter of a mile past the tent, you can see the foundation of what will be the largest chapel in the state, maybe even the country! That Chapel will replace the large tent when it's finished. Well, let's continue, shall we?"

They all climbed back into the tram as Rev. Smith explained to Sara, "Now you hold on tight, honey, because we're going to take this hill rather fast!"

When they were all safely in the tram, Charlie floored it, and they raced down the slope, bumping and laughing all the way!

When they reached the bottom, and continued at a more sensible rate of speed, Rev. Smith explained to the Crawfords the procedure used to verify healings at the Park.

"First, Sara will have to be taken to the medical tent, that large white one over there." He pointed to his left then continued, "After they verify her illness, she'll be assigned to a specific night in which to enter the meeting. This usually takes about two days or so. If the Lord grants your healing miracle, then we ask that you allow her to take the tests again so that we'll have the documentation we need to prove the healing. This cuts down on the accusations about fraudulent healings."

Rev. Smith noticed the Crawfords' disappointed looks when he mentioned the two or three day wait; so he said, "Look, I know you expected to just come here, get healed, and leave again, but I'm afraid it just doesn't work that way. We must follow these guidelines, but believe me, it'll be all right."

As they approached the medical tent, they saw a tall man, about six-feet three-inches, with a very lean and muscular frame and the whitest hair they'd ever seen.

The tram had barely stopped when Sara jumped out, ran up to the man shouting as she ran, "Mr. White, wait, please!"

The man turned, and Sara saw that he had exquisitely deep blue eyes. She ran and jumped into the surprised man's arms.

*　　*　　*

Joshua White had made his rounds in the hospital

ward and had received full reports on the twenty-five confirmed miracles from last night's meeting. His head was filled with pleasant thoughts as he entered the hot afternoon sun.

He was walking toward the chapel to pray when he heard someone yell, "Mr. White, wait, please!"

When he turned, sadness filled his heart. He saw a little girl running on wasted little legs. Her face was drawn tight across her cheekbones, and she had very little hair. He'd seen this far too often over the last two years. Most that entered in this condition left healthy, but some of them were buried in Jesus Park's new cemetery. Joshua almost didn't catch the girl as she threw herself into his arms with surprising strength. He hugged her, as if he'd known her all of her life, and she hugged him back.

She surprised Joshua again when she whispered in his ear, "Can you and Jesus heal my daddy of his drinking sickness so we can be happy again?"

Joshua whispered back, "I'll do my best, honey, I'll do my best."

As Joshua was setting Sara down on her own two feet, Rev. Smith ran up and said, "Sorry Josh, but Sara here is very anxious to be healed."

"No need to apologize, Pastor, I think she's sweet."

As the Crawfords came up, Rev. Smith introduced them to Joshua. Joshua assured them that he'd do his best for their little Sara. Rev. Smith took them back toward the medical tent's entrance.

Joshua continued his walk toward the Chapel; he had a lot of petitions to pray for this afternoon.

As he walked, he began to pray for Sara and her daddy, "Lord Jesus, I've just met the sweetest soul that I think I've ever met. Though she's riddled with, what I'll guess to be cancer of some kind, Sara just asked me to help her daddy with his drinking problem. She isn't even worried about herself. Oh Lord, if there could be more people like her, with a deep, selfless love for others; this world would be a much better place!

"Lord help her daddy, if it's your will to do so, and keep little Sara safe! Thank you!

"I also bring another matter before you, Jesus. Waiting in the Chapel tent, to which I'm now heading, is a delegation of ministers and doctors. Both groups have the same complaint... Jesus Park. I can already guess what they'll say and I understand their concerns, Jesus, but please help me to win them over to your work here, Lord, so they may become a part of all you are doing instead of being thorns.

"Well, Lord, I've arrived; please help my faith and increase my wisdom. Amen."

When Joshua entered the tent, he saw the small group of men and women standing in a small circle talking to one another. They stopped talking and moved into a straight line facing Joshua, as he walked down the center isle toward them. He recognized most of the twelve people, four ministers (three men and one woman), and the rest doctors. He'd had some heated debates with these twelve people over the last couple of years and he could only imagine what complaint they'd expound upon today.

Joshua smiled as he reached the group, and said, "Good afternoon ladies and gentlemen! Won't you have a seat?"

He received cold smiles, as Dr. Longshore stepped

forward, taking his usual position as spokesman for the group.

"We won't be staying long enough to sit, White. I guess you feel very smug now that you've won your abortion reprieve?!"

A joy began to stir in Joshua's heart, "My what?!"

"You heard me, White! Don't act like you don't know! The President just announced, on national television, that the Roe vs. Wade decision has just been overturned two hours ago!"

A couple of the woman doctors were wiping tears from there eyes, *"Sorrow over lost income, no doubt!"*, thought Joshua, but what he said was, "Actually, I hadn't heard the news yet, but I'm very happy for the innocent lives that'll be saved by this move of our new Supreme Court Justices."

Dr. Longshore's face was getting red a sign that he should check his own blood pressure once in awhile.

He said, "This isn't the only travesty of justice that I see for our immediate future! It's rumored that President Place has finally gotten enough votes to put prayer back in schools, the work places, and the government! She's even talking about using the Bible as a textbook in the public schools again, like it was when this country was founded! This is dangerous talk, White, and we're here to warn you not to stick your collective noses any further into our business than you already have! We'll take care of the President in next month's election; but since you're not elected to the position you hold, we haven't figured out how to get rid of you yet, Mr. White, but we will!"

Joshua's own face was beginning to get hot, as he

said, "Why can't you people just concede that the citizens of the United States want us to return to the days of decency, honesty, integrity, honor and above all, faith in God! They want the blessings of that age, and they're finally awake enough to get out there and make it happen! They know that our only chance is to elect people who are honest, and have a solid moral character like our original leaders!

"No, Dr. Longshore, you <u>will not</u> find a way to stop the swing back to what is right and decent. People have seen the ugly face of your new age movement and they've rejected it! President Place is still the favorite to win next month's election so don't get your hopes up yet!"

Dr. Vivian Hopper stepped forward and said, "You're causing the financial failure of the medical field just as you did the public schools! Once the President issued those vouchers, which allowed the government to pay for public or private schools, giving the choice to the parents as to where to send their children, it only took one year to cause the near collapse of the entire educational system. We feel forcing us to go along with these changes set us back one hundred years! Now you're endangering the hospitals and nursing homes with your incessant healings here at Jesus Park!"

"You now employ most of the local doctors and nurses out here, and have virtually shut down the local hospitals and clinics! People come here to get healed instead of coming to the medical profession, as they should! You fill them with false hope and..."

Joshua interrupted, "Now wait just a moment, Dr. Hopper! All of the healings that Jesus has done here have been medically recorded and documented by competent

Christian doctors! We've even tried to maintain a couple of atheist doctors on staff, out of fairness, but they convert to Christianity as fast as we can recruit them!"

"You, as I've said on several occasions, are welcome to come out and witness the entire procedure from start to finish and judge for yourself..."

Dr. Longshore's deep voice broke in, "We've already decided, White, and our consensus is that you're risking people's lives here and you should be shut down! On our way in here, we counted ten graves in the cemetery out there! Ten people that died because they came here, instead of seeking competent medical help!"

"No doctor, they came here because the medical profession told them there was no hope and they found peace here before the Lord took them home! I never promise that all will live that come here! That's for the Lord to decide! We do, however, treat the entire person, body, mind, and soul; you can't treat the one without treating the others!"

"President Place has been working on several proposals that'll help the medical profession in perfecting this lost art of treating the entire person!"

Dr. Hopper said, "We want you Christians to stay out of our business all together! You're going to ruin our country!".......'No, Dr. Hopper, that's already been done by your humanist agenda, we're simply trying to breathe life into the dead hulk you've left behind with the cancer of your hidden agenda!".......'Mr. White," Bishop Vokmer broke in, "As you know, it has been the tradition of our church to help people around the world, and we applaud your work and that of the President in bringing about the end of abortion! I must, however, agree with my friends here, that you have no training, no license, and no right, to perform these so called miracles! You're not even an ordained minister! You're an ex-cop and nothing more!

"It's the position of our church that we can't recognize a person's work just because he claims to know Jesus or the Holy Spirit. Your work must be approved by the proper authorities, or it must stop!"

Joshua looked from face to face and saw, to his dismay, total agreement.

With sadness Joshua said, "The ministers, priests, doctors and nurses who help me here are interested in the same thing that I am, the easing of human suffering, whether it be physical, mental or spiritual..."

Bishop Vokmer yelled, "There are no priests helping you here! The ones that refused to leave have been relieved of their priesthood!"

Joshua asked with a sinking heart, "Fr. Jerry Powell?".......Is now Mr. Powell, as far as we're concerned!", answered a very smug Bishop Vokmer.

Joshua shook his head sadly, and said, "I've repeatedly invited you to help and would be more than happy to have you join us. I will not, however, have you threatening the President, myself, or any of my helpers! You're all so full of self-interest, pride and hypocrisy that I don't believe you really see the suffering that's going on around you. You've spent so much time making sure everyone gets to do whatever they want to do that you haven't stopped to look at the consequences of your deadly philosophy!

"You're all going to have to face the fact that your way didn't work nor can it ever work! As long as the Lord tarries his return and the Christians remain in the world, we'll fight for the moral sanity of humans everywhere! There'll come a time when the Lord will come back and take the Christians out of the world. Then you and your kind will be cursed with running the world your way! For your sake, I truly hope you don't have to live through that tribulation period! Now if you'll excuse me, I have many things to pray about today, and you're at the top of my list!"

With that, Joshua turned his back on his visitors, knelt down, and began to pray.

The members of the Committee for the Preservation of the New Age Movement looked at each other, then at Joshua and then back to each other again. Anger welled up inside them because of Joshua's stinging words. Each wanted to rebuke him, yell at him, disprove what he'd said, but they knew that they couldn't. So instead, one by one, they silently turned and walked out of the tent, beaten again by this man's sincerity, integrity, and holiness.

*   *   *

Aaron laid a loving hand on Josh's shoulder, and smiled down at his human charge. He'd been Joshua's guardian angel for over forty years now, and had carried him through many dangers and temptations. Aaron was brilliant with the Glory of God; he'd just come from His presence. He had a message for Joshua from God, Himself, and he felt a mixture of pride, and sorrow for Joshua at this moment. Pride that God had chosen

Joshua for such important work, and sorrow that Joshua would have to suffer many persecutions to accomplish that work!

CHAPTER FOUR
ANGELS STRUGGLE DAILY

Sam Crawford was experiencing something that he'd forgotten existed, peace of mind and soul. There was something about these people that allowed him to relax. They made him feel important, like he really did matter, and they seemed so confident. Rev. Smith seemed to think that even the biggest of the Crawford's problems would turn out all right with God's help. The strange part was that Sam had come to believe it himself, well, almost anyway.

Sam, who had no way of knowing how to solve his present dilemma, felt a tinge of guilt at what he had been sent here to do by Creen. To kill an unknown human was bad enough, but to kill Rev. Smith, now that he'd met him, and after all the kindness he'd shown Sam's family; well, it was going to be very difficult, to say the least!

Rev. Smith held the tent flap open for Sam and Barb, and they entered their own personal tent.

He said, "I assure you that the hospital staff will take good care of Sara. They told me that they'll be doing tests until around 5:50 this afternoon at which time you can pick her up and go to supper."

"No Charge!" both he and Sam said at the same time. It had become a joke between them, and Rev. Smith was glad to see Sam lighten-up a little.

He continued with the tour of their tent, "As you can see, we've tried to give you all the comforts of home! The tents are made of a heavy canvas material, very

41

sturdy. We've provided wooden flooring throughout and in the living area, here, a couch, two recliners, with floor lamps, and even a small desk."

As Rev. Smith pointed to each of the items, proudly naming them, Sam reached for the plastic gun still held snugly under his shirt. *"No!"* he thought, *"I must wait until after Sara is healed, then I'll do it!"* Sam moved his hand away from his shirt.

The pastor then led them into the next room, which was a large bedroom. It had a double bed, dressing table with mirror, and a small refrigerator. The next room, located off of the bedroom, was about half its size, had a single bed, and a small dresser. Sam and Barb looked at each other and smiled. It seemed that this tent was built just for them and it gave them a warm feeling.

Rev. Smith studied the Crawfords for a minute and then asked, "Is it to your liking?"

Barb kissed him on the cheek and said, "Oh yes, thank you!"

Even Sam, despite what he was about to do, shook the Pastor's hand with feeling and showed none of the earlier jealousy or hatred.

Sam thought, *"I don't know if I can kill this man, debt or no debt! He's been so helpful and he seems so sincere,"* but, what he said was, "I want to thank you for all of your help this morning! You've come to us just like the angels did in the stories that my mother read to me as a boy. In this place, I almost believe they could be real!"

Rev. Smith said, "Sam, they're real all right, as you'll discover for yourself while you're here. For now, however, I suggest you get a couple of hours sleep."

Re-entering their bedroom, Rev. Smith took the

alarm clock out of a drawer in the dresser, set it and handed it to Sam.

"I've set it for about two and half hours. This'll give you plenty of time to pick Sara up and then go eat. I really hope you enjoy your stay here; and if you ever need anything, just ask for me and I'll see what I can do."

Sam said, with a growing respect, "Thanks, again, Pastor Smith."

After the Pastor left, Sam turned to Barb, and said, "Do you really believe these people can save Sara?"

Barb looked at him and said, in almost a whisper, "I hope so, Sam, I really do hope so!"

Sam was still holding the alarm clock that Rev. Smith had given him as he left the tent; so he put it down on the desk in the living room, and then flopped into one of the recliners with a sigh. Barb did likewise and they were both asleep in a couple of heartbeats.

Hosterian bent down, placed an angelic hand on Sam's forehead and blessed him. The angel looked as though he'd fallen into a vat of acid. The tip of his right wing was severed; both wings were full of holes from the demon's acidic spittle, and he had a deep gash in his forehead, which had long since clotted and dried over.

The last battle with the demons, just before entering Jesus Park's hedge of protection, had been a fierce one; a battle which had cost Hosterian his sword, when it had snapped in two, as he severed the head of an extraordinarily strong demon.

He looked over at Lutrinda, who was blessing Barb in the same manner, and he noticed that Lutrinda hadn't fared much better. Those demons hadn't wanted to lose the Crawfords; they'd invested a lot of effort in the damning of their souls.

Just then, Andy flew into the tent and said to the others, "Sara's safe for the moment. Yours?"

Andy nodded to the sleeping parents of his charge. His friends nodded affirmative.

He continued, "Now would be a good time to report to Michael and get you two healed up before we have to report back here!"

Hosterian and Lutrinda had looked up as Andy flew in and had just shaken their heads. He didn't have a scratch on him. Oh, he'd had to ward off a few demons, but none of them had any real claim on Sara making his passage a lot easier. As one, the three angels took flight and entered the life giving presence of their God.

*   *   *

Joshua White lay prostrate before his God in deep contemplation. He was in the midst of a terrifying vision, when Ellen White entered the tent. Ellen couldn't, of course, see Aaron who knelt next to Joshua but she could see the results of the vision that Aaron imparted to Joshua.

Ellen watched as Joshua struggled with this vision, for what seemed the hundredth time. Ellen had, of course, known Joshua all of her life and hoped to marry him at one time but had married his brother, Chad, instead. Two years ago, however, she'd found out that Chad was involved with the witches in the area and on that same day his own fellow warlocks had murdered him. Ellen had mourned the loss of her husband, even though he'd been abusive and unfaithful, but over these past two years she and Joshua had grown much closer.

They enjoyed the same things and, of course, worshipped together almost daily. As Joshua had taken more and more upon himself, Ellen had begun to take care of him making sure that he ate and rested on a, somewhat, regular schedule. The man would forget to take care of himself at all if she didn't remind him. She was disturbed by this recurring vision but found she was smiling in spite of her feelings. She was becoming more and more aware that she loved this man who lay before her in the dirt. She recognized the loving, selfless soul that dwelt in his heart and she loved his gentle ways. She longed for the day that he'd propose marriage but understood his preoccupation with his work.

Ellen looked at her watch, and whispered, "Oh my! We have to leave now if Josh is to get cleaned up, fed, and back here for tonight's meeting."

She walked over to Joshua, knelt down, and gently shook his shoulder.

Joshua found himself locked into the same horrifying vision that he'd experienced so many times over the last month or so. He'd promised to take this vision to Granny Girard, who has the gift of interpreting dreams and visions, but he'd never managed to find the time.

Joshua braced himself as the dark cloud descended over the United States and he almost screamed when he saw the evil demons swirling within the cloud. The ground beneath the feet of the citizens turned to quicksand and slowly, millions of thrashing, screaming, men, women, and children sank out of sight, below the surface.

Then, again, from the surface of the earth rose, first the American flag, and then the dome of the White House on which it flew. As the flag touched the dark cloud, it reluctantly gave way to the bright sunlight.

The first time Joshua had witnessed this part of the vision he'd felt joy, but now he only felt horror at what was to come. The expected shadow rose up from behind the White House. It was a very large demon with bright, red eyes, and hungry, rotting teeth. He raised his sword and, with one powerful blow, cut the dome free from the White House. The demon ducked as a bright bolt of lightening raced toward him but once it was spent all was dark again, and the newly rent dome quickly filled with quicksand, and was once again submerged below the now smooth surface of the earth.

The demon then turned toward Joshua, opened its mouth, which continued to grow wider and closer until it dropped from above, enveloping him with a stifling darkness. Fear, hopelessness, and unspeakable evil threatened to take total control...

Joshua jumped and as he rolled over onto his back, acrid sweat ran from his brow into his now open eyes, which caused them to burn. Through his blurred vision, he saw Ellen's concerned face looking down at him. As his vision cleared, Joshua could see the warm, kind soul of Ellen looking out of her beautiful blue eyes. Her brilliant, shimmering, brown hair flowed down and around Ellen's shoulders as she knelt next to him.

Ellen put on her most scolding face and said, "You were having that vision again weren't you?"

With Ellen's help, Joshua stood and stretched his aching muscles, saying through a sigh, "Yes, I'm afraid I was. I'm going to have to ask Granny what she makes of it."

Ellen took his arm saying, "You're coming with me mister!"

She pointed as Joshua opened his mouth to protest, "No arguments now. You can ask Granny tomorrow; but for now, you're going to get cleaned up, get some rest, and then I'll feed you a nice supper."

As if on cue, Josh's stomach growled and he said, "Well, I guess I'm out voted on this one!"

They both laughed, as Joshua put his arm around Ellen's waist, and they left the tent together. As they walked toward her car laughing and joking as was their habit, neither of them noticed the evil chill that was permeating the afternoon air around them.

*   *   *

Grady stuck his head out of the shower thinking he'd heard the phone ringing. He was just pulling the curtain closed when he heard it again. Jumping out of the shower, he grabbed a towel, and ran down the hallway dripping water on the floor as he went. He grabbed the phone with his left hand and tried to tie the towel with his right exclaiming into the phone, "Oh, my heavens! Hold on please!"

Grady put the receiver down, retrieved the towel from the floor and wrapped it around himself again this time using both hands to secure it.

He picked up the phone again, "Hello, you there?"

Grady was wet, cold, and just a little irritated.

"Grady? Is that you, honey?"

"Marla! Hi! I didn't think you were calling until tomorrow! How's Washington?"

"Grady! What's wrong? You're out of breath, you dropped the receiver, right in my ear I might add, and..."

"I'm sorry about that, honey. I was in the shower when you called; and as I ran down the hall, I had a little trouble with my towel and it..."

"All right!" Marla laughed, "I get the picture, sweetheart. Listen, I've got some great news! I'm flying in tomorrow morning at 5:00 and I need you to pick me up. Can you do that?"

"Of course I can! It'll be great to see you, honey! Marla, really though, you have to tell me why the sudden change in plans? Does it have to do with the great news I heard today about the abortion decision being reversed by the Supreme Court?"

"Grady I can't tell you over the phone. There's too much, well, espionage going on around here. President Place advised me not to say too much over the phone, but I promise to fill you in when I get there."

"Are you in any danger, Marla? I can come..."

"That's sweet, Grady, but you know that Killer is never too far away. He won't let anything happen to me. He'll put me on the plane tomorrow and you'll be at the other end to meet me so what can happen? I have to run, Grady, but be there at 5:00 sharp!"

"I will Marla and Marla?"

"Yes Grady?"

"After you tell me this secret news of yours, I want

to discuss our wedding date. I think it's time that we get serious about it, don't you?"

"Oh Grady! That'll be wonderful! I can't wait until our wedding night!"

"Marla Brinkle! You're terrible! However, I have to agree with you, because I can't wait either! I'm glad we waited for our wedding night though; it'll mean so much more to us then. Well, I'll see you in the morning honey."

"Let's at least have a good night kiss, shall we Grady?"

"I don't know, Marla, what would people think if they saw the world's greatest anchor woman kissing a phone?"

"They'd say that she must be madly in love with her man, that's what!"

They laughed, put their lips to the phone receiver and smacked them together several times. Each longed to hold the other in their arms. They were both smiling when they hung up.

Grady smiled feeling warm inside. He really missed Marla and couldn't wait to see her in the morning.

His thoughts turned to Killer, which made his smile broaden. Killer, whose real name was Harold Barber, was a big man heavily tattooed with a long, shaggy beard, long black hair and a heart of gold. He was the President of the "Angels", a Christian motorcycle gang that had taken on the task of security for the workers at Jesus Park. Grady knew that Killer wouldn't let anything happen to Marla and that made him feel better. Killer was the man who'd transported Marla safely to the Capitol during the Battle of Covenant and he'd been protecting her ever since. Grady was disturbed, just a little, about this talk of spies and secrets but he figured that Marla and President Place were probably just being overly cautious.

The running water in the bathroom reminded Grady that he had a shower to finish before work. Only happy thoughts filled Grady's mind as he re-entered his shower.

Grady couldn't see Warren, his guardian angel, as he drew his sword, nor did he feel the uneasiness, which suddenly filled the mighty angel with dread.

In a van outside of Grady's apartment, a man wearing earphones placed the listening device on the desk in front of him, turned to his partner saying, "She's coming in on the 5:00 a.m. flight."

His partner picked up the phone, scrambled it, and then dialed the unlisted number of his master.

CHAPTER FIVE
OPERATION CLEANSE

Rev. Smith was wearing jeans and a **"Jesus Park"** T-shirt. He very seldom dressed in suits anymore, because his duties were mainly background preparations. He handled things such as, getting ready for the meetings that Joshua conducted. As a matter of fact, the Pastor had just finished the chore of assigning places to the twenty volunteer ministers for this evenings meeting.

Rev. Smith opened his briefcase and while rummaging around looking for the extra copy of the volunteer list that he'd placed there earlier, he ran across a piece of his old stationary. It read, **THE CHURCH OF GRACE, REV. JOHNATHON SMITH, PASTOR.** His smile broadened as he thought about the changes God had wrought in his life over the last few years. He'd been pastor of the church for about seven years before the Battle of Covenant. Even as a pastor he'd grown in his Christian faith, by watching Joshua White humbly work for his God. He'd come to look at life very differently over the past two years. His position as manager of Jesus Park evolved during that period of time and had tested the humility of his spirit.

He laughed and whispered to himself, "I've gone from being Josh's pastor to being his helper."

He felt no bitterness; on the contrary, he was very comfortable with this arrangement.

As he placed the paper back in the briefcase, he prayed: "Lord, I want to thank you for guiding me in your

51

ways. This ministry is much more fulfilling than just being pastor of a church. I'm glad that you helped my congregation and myself to see the wisdom of Josh's suggestion, to close our church and move out here to Jesus Park. The revival, the miracles, and the kindness that we've experienced over the past two years have been glorious. Thank you!"

He shook his head at the memory of how the ministry had grown in leaps and bounds once they'd all committed their collective skills and gave it their full devotion. The number of volunteers, both ministers and lay people, seems to increase daily. People, once touched by the Lord's kindness, wanted to return it, in some way, to others. Their best outlet was to help others experience that same love through prayer and healing meetings.

The pastor looked around. Everything seemed ready. Just then, the silence of the tent was shattered by the static of his pack radio, "Hey Pastor, this is Hank at the North gate. Can I let the people in or not?"

Rev. Smith smiled, remembering the argument that had occurred between Joshua and the security chief (that was insisted on by the Covenant City Fathers, which Joshua strongly objected to and eventually capitulated) before "the North gate" had even been created. Security insisted that they needed a ten foot razor wire topped fence all around Jesus Park and then another around the meeting tent itself. Joshua had laughed scornfully and said, "I have already been murdered and brought back from the dead! What need do I have of a security fence or any security for that matter! My God is big enough to protect me!"

Joshua had started to walk away from the Security

Chief, the matter settled as far as he was concerned, but stopped dead in his tracks when the security chief yelled, "Thou shalt not tempt the Lord your God!" The discussion continued for another two hours until Joshua finally compromised, "For the safety of the people", and allowed a security fence and gate to be constructed around the chapel tent only saying, "I will not have Jesus Park looking like a concentration camp as the pilgrims pull up!" Nothing had been said about the metal detector so the Chief just installed one as a matter of course and it was a grumpy Joshua White who let it stand.

Rev. Smith chuckled as he grabbed his own mike and said, "Yes Hank, go ahead. I believe we're set."

When the gates of the chain-link fence, which surrounded the chapel tent, opened Sam Crawford picked up Sara and followed Barb through the metal detector gates. It hadn't taken the normal two days to get invited to a meeting thanks to Rev. Smith's persistence. He'd told the medical staff to push Sara's tests through and get them into tonight's meeting.

Sam and Barb were ecstatic when they got the word to come to tonight's meeting. Even though the doctors had verified the bad news that Sara was, indeed, dying of an inoperable metastasized cancerous brain tumor, they were hopeful for a cure. Sam, however, could've done without the stress of reliving the painful facts of his daughter's illness. Oh, the doctors and nurses were kind and loving people and they'd explained that the tests were necessary in order to authenticate the miracle of their daughter's cure, but it was still stressful to the parents and Sam thought, *"I really need a drink!"*

He put that thought aside as their turn had finally

arrived to enter one of these highly recommended prayer meetings and they'd soon see if this talk of miracles was true.

Sam was surprised at all the security precautions taking place. They'd just passed through a metal detector like those seen at an airport. They were about to be patted down by security people, saying they were looking for plastic weapons. Sam held Sara close to him and he felt the hard object next to his heart. The security officer, seeing the little girl's condition and the fact that there hadn't been any incidents in the two year operation of Jesus Park, didn't ask him to move his daughter; therefore, not finding the thing hidden under Sam's shirt.

It was a beautiful fall evening, not too hot or too cold. Sam even noticed that there were no mosquitoes or other pesky insects flying around, except high up around the flood lights that had just come on. The Crawfords had been first in line and were ushered right up front. Barb and Sara were excited, laughing and enjoying the sights. They watched the many types of people who entered the tent after them. Sam, for his part, just looked straight ahead watching Rev. Smith and the security people going through their tasks in the speaker's area of the tent. He was very distracted and nervous.

Sam wasn't really sure about all of this God stuff. He'd felt something when they first arrived, but that had worn off quickly. Now he was only going through the motions, hoping against hope that if there was a God, he would have mercy on his daughter despite his own sinful intentions. Sam looked down at Sara and watched her hopeful face glow with a youthful faith--a faith that made his own anger grow!

He thought, *"What's happened to my own youthful faith?"*

Sam had been eight years old when he saw his father beat his mother to death. His mother had been the kindest person in the world. She always knew how to make Sam feel better and she always did her best to protect him when his father came home in one of his drunken stupors.

On one particular night when his father arrived home, Sam had run up to him all excited about the science project that he and his mother had just finished. It had taken them three weeks to complete and he just knew that he'd get an "A", when he turned in the assignment.

His father had looked down at him irritably and shoved him out of the way. Sam had staggered backward, falling over a footstool that caused his project to fly into the air and when it came down it shattered in a million painful pieces. It not only cut Sam's skin; but also cut deeply into his heart. Sam's father kicked him in the stomach for making a mess. When Sam's mother tried to stop him, his father turned his attention on her. What he did to her, right in front of Sam, was forever etched into Sam's soul.

When Sam's father knocked his mother to the kitchen floor and proceeded to beat her, Sam had prayed that God would stop him; "Make him have a heart attack and die, or something. Just stop him God!"

God didn't stop him, however and by the time his father had finished, Sam's mother was lying dead on the kitchen floor. When Sam's prayer didn't work, he crawled to the phone and dialed the police. They arrived just as

Sam's father was bringing a knife down with the intent of piercing Sam's already broken heart.

The police officer had shouted, "Freeze mister! Police!"

Then two shots rang out and blood splattered across Sam's face. As his father fell on top of him, Sam felt the warm blood on his skin as it soaked through his clothing. Sam found himself delighted when his father's last alcohol-ridden breath gurgled into Sam's tear stained face. The tears had been for his mother not his father. That had been the last day that Sam had prayed to his mother's God; a God that had let them both down.

Sam's reverie was interrupted when a wheelchair bumped into his own seat. Sam had tears running down his face when he looked to his right and saw, to his horror, a shriveled child sitting in the wheelchair next to him. He gasped at the poor child whose shrunken leathery skin was stretched tightly over his skull looked like a sick replica of Sam at that age.

The child looked up at him and said, "Don't worry Sam! God loves you and you'll see your mother again someday. She's happy and loved where she is!"

Sam cried out and hit Barb's arm. He wanted her to see this child, but when they turned back and he pointed, the child was gone--wheelchair and all. Sam was shaking, both from the bad memory and from this strange experience, when Rev. Smith called the meeting to order.

*   *   *

The man's heart was racing when he put the receiver down. They'd moved the van so that Grady wouldn't see it. The man who'd been using the listening device was now driving slowly down 32nd Street. They were approaching the nice neighborhood in which Joshua White lived. The driver watched the people as he passed by them. He watched as happy couples cooked their suppers on grills in their driveways or shot baskets with their kids or washed the car together or even mowed their lawns. All these and many more activities could be seen as he drove by. He longed for the time to be with his own family. He longed for a normal life where he wouldn't have to worry about national security or the end of the world. When you're in the Central Intelligence Agency; however, your time isn't your own it belongs to your government!

The driver's reverie was broken as his excited partner replaced the phone in its cradle and exclaimed, "We're to initiate 'Operation Cleanse' immediately!"

The men smiled at each other glad to finally be getting some action. The driver picked up the mike of his radio and said into the secured communications link, "All units! Alert Z-2! I repeat, Alert Z-2! Operation Cleanse in five, four, three, two, one, mark!"

Powerful forces, coiled like a snake poised to strike, sprang into action. Within seconds they converged upon and surrounded the unsuspecting occupants of Joshua White's home.

CHAPTER SIX

THE ABDUCTION

As Rev. Smith walked up to the microphones, his stomach began to knot. Josh had never been this late before and the Pastor wasn't ready to run a meeting by himself. He, just that moment, realized how much he'd taken Joshua for granted. He'd grown comfortable with the fact that Joshua would always be here to do the praying and talking so the pastor could hide in the relative safety of the background chores. Now, however, it seemed that Rev. Smith was being thrown into the spotlight whether he liked it or not.

His head throbbed, as he remembered what Josh had told him many times recently, "If, for some reason I'm unable to attend one of these meetings, Pastor; I expect you to run it in my absence. Your faith is just as strong as mine and, after all, it's the power of Jesus that does the saving and the healing! So just step out in faith and let the Holy Spirit do His job!" The Pastor had always agreed, rather lightly, never thinking that he'd have to carry it through. Now, here it was staring him right in the face. His conscience scolded him, *"Look, mister! You've been a pastor for years, surely you can pray for healing in faith and leave the results up to Jesus!"*

It didn't help. The butterflies in his stomach were still flying around wildly, and his head was about to explode with pain! As Rev. Smith began to speak, the crowd became suddenly very quiet and all of those hopeful eyes were now on him.

He bowed his head and said, "Let us pray. Lord Jesus! There's no other name in heaven or on earth or in hell that's more powerful than your name! Lord Jesus Christ, it's in your powerful name that we gather this day! I ask you, Lord, to station your powerful angels around us today. Have them cast out the demons from among us under the authority of Jesus' name! May they then stand guard with their swords drawn ready to fight the demons of darkness that will try to stop today's message from reaching our hearts and changing our lives!"

"You told us, Lord, in your Holy Scriptures that where two or more are gathered in your name you are there also. Well Jesus, we're gathered in your name, we know through faith that you're indeed present with us and that you're just as powerful today as you were when you walked among us! We have faith in your healing power Lord; the power to heal our bodies, our minds and yes, even our souls!"

"Jesus, the world tells us that there's no real power in your name. The world tells us that we should count on our own power or cosmic power or the stars or even the universal force, but these are but shadows compared to the glory and power of You, God, and Your Son, Jesus Christ!"

"So for today Lord, we'll cast out all doubt from our hearts and we'll stand in your mighty presence, in awe of our mighty God! We'll enjoy the blessings that you're about to pour out on us in your abundance! We promise this in the name of your Son, Jesus Christ, our Savior and Lord! Amen!"

The pastor looked again into the hopeful faces of

the assembled crowd. What should he tell them? He remembered what Josh had always said, "Speak in truth and faith and the rest will take care of itself."

Rev. Smith took a deep breath and said, "We've gathered today to honor our God with faith! We'll share the many miracles that have already been done in His Wonderful Name and then we'll watch in awe as new miracles will, most assuredly, happen here tonight!"

Thunderous applause rocked the grounds of Jesus Park as every one of the ten thousand souls present felt the Spirit of God stir among them.

Rev. Smith shouted into the lull that followed, "How many here believe in the power of our God?"

There was more applause and shouted agreements as many of the believers stood. His confidence soared as the Holy Spirit filled his heart and soul.

The pastor continued with a more peaceful heart, "After our opening song, we'll testify to the greatness of our God and then we'll ask him to bless us. We'll ask him to heal our sick, to cast out demons and to save our souls from the Evil One!"

In the applause that followed, he turned to the music director and gave him the signal to begin. As the pastor sat down he prayed that Josh would hurry up and get here.

He whispered to himself, "Where are you Joshua?"

*   *   *

Joshua White felt rested and hungry. He found himself laying under the covers of his bed his foggy memory coming back to him slowly.

Ellen had driven him home and while he'd taken a long relaxing shower, she'd laid out his pajamas. He'd just slipped into them when Ellen had knocked on the door, peeked in and smiled. He slipped under the covers, laid back and barely remembered her kiss on his cheek; for there's no memory of events from that moment until this.

Josh could smell fried chicken and that set his stomach to rumbling. He got up, took off his pajamas and put on his suit pants and a T-shirt. He went into the bathroom, brushed his teeth, then his hair. He slipped into his white dress shirt and after tucking it in, entered the hallway. He could hear the sizzling of the chicken as it deep fried and the aroma grew more heavenly the closer he got to it's source. Walking into the kitchen, he saw Ellen dancing around getting the meal ready. She had a Walkman clipped to the belt of her dress and headphones hugged her ears.

Joshua smiled at this happy and generous soul. It was at moments like this, he knew beyond a shadow of a doubt, he was to marry this woman. He also knew that he could wait no longer, in that he longed to share his life with her. Joshua slipped up behind Ellen and put his arms around her waist pulling her to him as he did so.

Ellen jumped and exclaimed as she looked back to see who it was, "Oh! Oh, Joshua White! You startled me!"

She took off the headphones, turned in his arms and they kissed.

While they were hugging, Ellen whispered into Josh's ear, "Do you feel any better, honey?"

Joshua held her out at arms length and said, "I feel

wonderful, thanks to you! I'll feel even better when I get some of this food into me. It looks like you've out done yourself again!"

Ellen blushed with pleasure and said, "Well, just have a seat and I'll bring it right out!"

He reluctantly let her go, leaned against the wall and watched Ellen work. He put his hand in his pocket and felt the velvet box.

After another couple minutes of thought he said, "Ellen, I have something to ask you."

Ellen looked up from her efforts at mashing potatoes and said, "What is it honey?"

"Well, you know that I've been rather distracted lately, and well I've taken way too long for this!"

He stepped up to her and knelt down on his right knee. As Ellen looked down at him, her mouth fell open. Josh took the box out of his pocket and opened it.

He held the ring up and said, "Ellen, would you please marry me and soon?!"

Ellen screamed, "Yes! Yes! Oh yes!", as she jumped up and down.

Joshua slipped the ring on her finger as Ellen knelt down in front of him. They hugged and kissed. Then Ellen held her hand out and admired the ring.

She said, "It's beautiful honey! I love you very much!"

She gave him another hug and kiss, then got up to finish supper. Josh got up and rubbed her shoulders thanking God silently for the gift of allowing him to have two wonderful women in his life Patricia, his first wife who'd died several years ago, and now Ellen.

Joshua's thoughts turned to when he'd been shot

and died of his wounds. Had it just been two years ago? He smiled at the thought of his meeting with Jesus and how he'd been allowed to spend an entire day with his long dead wife, Patricia. That had been a wonderful day! That same day Patricia had told him that Ellen was in love with him, and that when she was free to marry, as she soon would be, Josh had to promise that he'd propose to Ellen and get married. Patricia hadn't wanted him to be lonely any longer. Shortly after that, Jesus had brought Josh back to life in time to lead his brother, Chad, to the Lord before he was shot and killed by Asst. Chief Anderson, who in turn had been killed.

Josh had helped Ellen through her grief and she, in turn, had helped him through his.

"Actually", he thought, *"the past two years have been one of the happiest times of my life! I just wish we hadn't waited so long..."*

"Josh!", Ellen laughed, "You're daydreaming again!"

"I was just thinking about how blessed I am! I've had a wonderful life and am about to start an entirely new one with you! Who could ask for more than that?"

Ellen smiled with pleasure as she looked at her watch and exclaimed, "Oh my! We have to leave in forty-five minutes for the meeting. Let's sit down and eat before it gets cold."

Together they placed the meal on the table, dished it up on their plates and then said grace. During the meal they happily made plans for their upcoming wedding.

The leader of the black clad unit gave the signal to wait. These men made up the best Cleansing Unit that the CIA had ever produced. They'd assassinated

Presidents and other highly placed government officials. They'd kidnapped key political leaders from every government in the world, including their own, then had taken these men and women to a secret brainwashing mental hospital located some one-hundred and fifty yards beneath the "Blue Skies Veterans Hospital". This secret CIA installation had turned out many mental puppets, who once brainwashed was then sent back to their jobs to carry out their programmed tasks. It's to this secret installation that the team was instructed to take Joshua White.

The leader looked at his watch; six twenty-nine. One more minute and they'd strike. He watched, hungrily, almost jealously, as Joshua finished off his chicken, mashed potatoes and gravy. Then, he drooled as Joshua ate what looked to be a very good piece of apple pie.

The black-gloved hand went up into the air and when it came down, five shadows entered the doors and windows of Joshua's house as if they didn't exist.

*　　*　　*

As Rev. Smith sat down and asked himself where Josh was, there was a commotion in the rear of the tent. Someone screamed and the crowd began to part. Rev. Smith was suddenly on his feet and walking toward the back of the tent. He stopped and gasped when he saw Grady, helping Ellen stagger through the crowd and he took note of her battered condition. Her long hair, which was normally very neat, was now out of place and flowing over her left shoulder, while hanging half down on her right. Her right cheek was swollen, turning a bluish color. Her right eye was all but closed and her lips still had dried blood on them. Her dress sleeves were torn and her shoes were gone. Rev. Smith ran to them. As he got closer he could see that Ellen also had four deep gashes in her left arm where someone had clawed her with his fingernails. Rev. Smith held her trembling body to his as she began to sob heavily. He'd been her pastor for years now and he thought of her as a sister.

He stroked her hair and said, "It's all right, Ellen. Shush, now. Tell me what happened."

She fiercely wiped at her eyes with the handkerchief he'd offered her, then blew her nose angrily, grimacing at the pain it caused.

Through her angry, frustrated sobs, Ellen tried to explain what had happened, "They took him pastor!" As if in a trance she whispered, "In broad daylight, they came in like ghosts and took him!"

Ellen shuddered all over and then snapped out of it saying, "Oh, he fought! You wouldn't believe the things Josh can do! I've never seen anyone fight like he did. I think he would've bested them all except that one of them hit me in the face with his rifle and started to rip my dress. Josh was distracted by this just long enough for another man to hit him from behind!"

As he staggered forward, Josh shouted, "Tell Granny Girard about the dream Ellen!"

"That's all he could say before the man hit him again. Then the man who was on top of me hit my face several times and when I woke up Grady was opening the front door. He'd seen that my car was still in the drive and stopped to check on us. We searched the house but there was no sign of Josh anywhere."

Ellen began to shudder again, her voice dropped to a whisper as she repeated, "They came and went just like ghosts, pastor! Why would they take him? Where would they take him?"

Ellen began to sob uncontrollably!

The pastor held her and whispered, "I don't know, Ellen. I just don't know!

CHAPTER SEVEN
AARON PETITIONS JESUS

Tumult jumped up and down with glee! He rubbed his hands together and basked in the warmth of his success. He couldn't believe how easy it had been. Aaron had left Joshua White helpless. Tumult and his demons had no trouble leading their human hosts to Joshua's location and even less trouble apprehending him.

Tumult passed out promotions to the demons that had helped with the operation. He then dismissed them and sneered with delight at the helpless form of Joshua White. Joshua's angelic defenders had finally lost interest in him, as Tumult knew they would; and he was about to take full advantage of the opportunity to mold Joshua White's future.

Tumult flashed into the air racing toward his destination at the speed of light; thinking as he went, *"Yes, Joshua's future! A future full of pain, hopelessness, fear and failure!"*

Rev. Smith remembered the crowd of people in the tent and his responsibility to them. He gently moved Ellen from his chest to his side and with his arm still around her; he led her toward the front of the tent. Grady followed close behind, as the silent crowd watched, wide-eyed, as they passed. The pastor passed Ellen over to Grady then stepped up to the microphone.

He looked at the faces of the crowd, and then answered their unspoken question, "Friends! The enemy has yet again, struck down Joshua White! They've taken him by force, but we have no idea as to whom, why or where they've taken him. Pray with me now! Let us ask our God to protect him in this new danger."

The crowd bowed their heads and a murmur arose from among them. It was a mournful sound that rose, even unto heaven...

Aaron angrily paced back and forth in front of the tent in which the Christians were, so painfully, praying for Josh's release. He had never liked orders that told him to back off and let the enemy in! He wanted Joshua back! He would, of course, do whatever Jesus ordered. Most assuredly, as an angel, it _was_ his duty to take the prayers of this crowd to the ear of the Lord.

In a flash, as bright as a star going nova, indicating the intensity of Aaron's angelic anger and frustration, he sped toward heaven to petition the Lord on behalf of these fine Christians! When he arrived, he found the Lord welcoming a new arrival, John Martin. John had been an ironworker, husband, father of four children, as well as a grandfather of seven. John had only five more years till retirement; when on this very day he had saved his fellow worker, Lisa. She'd slipped from the edge of the large steel beam located on the 32nd floor of the new high-rise they were building. As she began to fall, John pulled her to safety losing his own footing in the process and falling to his death.

Jesus was hugging John as he said; "There is no better gift, John, than to give your life for someone else!"

John looked up, with tear stained cheeks, and said, "Yes Lord, I know, but what of Sussie, our children and our grandchildren? What'll happen to them now?"

Jesus looked into John's face and smiled as he

replied, "They'll be looked after by me, as they've always been."

John was silent. A smile slowly appeared on his face, as he finally understood what life and death were all about. Gone were the fear and frustration and in their place were peace and joy.

Jesus turned to John's angel, "Cruacian, please take John to the home I've, personally, prepared for him and help him get settled. Then report to Michael for your new assignment."

Cruacian saluted then left with John.

Jesus then turned to Aaron, who immediately bowed before his Lord, saying, "I bring you the sad news that Joshua's been taken as anticipated and the hearts of the Christians are breaking, *again*!"

He put a lot of emphasis on that last word.

Jesus smiled down at Aaron saying, "Arise, Aaron, and walk with me."

As they walked the golden streets of "New Jerusalem", Jesus waved and smiled at the happy souls who were fulfilling their many duties and enjoying their many rewards.

Jesus said, "Aaron, you really like Josh don't you?"

Aaron agreed, "Yes Lord! I respect any warrior who's shown the faith, courage and heart that Josh has."

Jesus said, "Do you remember when Michael, Gabriel, Worl and many other angels, including yourself, cried out to My Father when I was taken prisoner on earth then led to My death on the cross?"

Aaron bowed his head, "Yes, I remember Lord."

Jesus stopped, placed both hands on Aaron's shoulders, turned Aaron to face him and said, "Aaron, I

71

had to be delivered into the hands of the enemy so that I could die for the sins of the entire human race! If I had called for help, every angel present would've come to my rescue and could have easily freed me. In doing so, however, we would have gone against my Father's Will and thus doomed the human race to an eternity in Hell with Satan!

"This trouble with Josh is also My Father's Will, Aaron! Would you go against that Will to save this brave human?"

Aaron shouted louder than he'd intended, "No, of course not, Lord!"

Jesus smiled, "Aaron, you're a faithful servant of the Throne of Heaven, and I know you'll do well. Do not fear my friend! Josh's faith runs deep and isn't dependent on miracles, comfort or ease! He still has the Holy Spirit to guide him on his way, and I'm confident that he'll prove himself worthy till the end!

"Aaron! There are great plans in the works, and only My Father, the Spirit and Myself know the outcome. Trust Us, Aaron, to know what's best in the lives of our creations--these humans. They still don't understand that life was never meant to be perfect without pain or suffering. These are things that once overcome, lead to happiness and contentment. Now let's put all doubt aside and discuss the next step in our plans..."

CHAPTER EIGHT
OLD ENEMIES-NEW FEARS

Joshua White fought the reflex to jump when he became conscious and found that he was lying on his stomach, with his face against the cold metal deck... of a helicopter? His trained senses detected four other men in the hold with him. Two were sitting on his right, the others on his left. The fog was beginning to clear from his brain, and he fought hard to remember what had happened.

Then the thoughts flooded together as if they'd been damned up then suddenly released in a torrent; Ellen, dinner, getting ready for the meeting, then the attack. He'd recognized the special forces brand of attack immediately, having been one himself for three years during his tour of duty in the army, then later in the secret "Cleanse" operation. These tactics were only used by the "Cleanse Force", which led Josh to believe that he'd been abducted by his own government. A feeling of betrayal sliced through his heart as he imagined his friend and President, Roberta Place, sending the unit after him; for only the President could authorize the use of **"Cleanse Force"**!

"No!", his thoughts scolded him, *"Roberta doesn't know about this operation. She could no more do this than she could kill someone!"*

Josh calmed himself with that thought and stifled the need to cough. He wanted to stay awake as long as they'd let him, so he acted as if he still slept while mentally recalling every detail of the attack.

They had suddenly burst into the house from every direction in a coordinated strike. Ellen had screamed, while Josh reacted as he had many times before. He always marveled at how his training came back to him during life threatening situations such as this one. He remembered hurting several of his attackers until one of them attacked Ellen, distracting him long enough to allow an assailant to strike him on the head, which was the last thing he remembered before darkness overcame him!

His plan now was to fake unconsciousness until they landed, then try to escape. This, too, was a reflex from his training.

One of the men spoke up, "Sir! It's time!"

"Then give him the shot. We wouldn't want to lose our prize now, would we?"

Josh felt the sting of the needle as it entered his thigh, just as his consciousness began to fade out again, he whispered, "I know that voice. I thought..."

The black-gloved man leaned forward and laughed, as he said to the again unconscious Joshua White, "Yes, my friend, you thought that you'd killed me but you were wrong and now you will pay!"

Tumult formed an unnatural sneer on the man's face and added an inhuman laugh, which escaped from deep within his possessed body, as the helicopter continued to race toward its destination.

*   *   *

As the prayers for Josh ended and more and more people looked to Rev. Smith for guidance, he looked from one expectant face to another wishing to say the right thing. Most of these people had come to see Joshua White, the famous miracle worker! They'd come in hopes of getting a cure for themselves or their loved ones, but now their hopes had been smashed or had they?

The Pastor cleared his throat, then spoke with much more confidence than he felt, "Even though Josh is gone and can't conduct this meeting, I feel that we should go on as usual!"

Murmuring rose from the crowd, "It was Josh who healed, what can you do?" and many other variations of that same statement.

Rev. Smith said, "Josh told me that if for any reason he couldn't be here, I was to conduct the meetings just as he had done! Josh reminded me, when I protested as you are, that it's not he who does the miracles but rather Jesus Christ who does them through the faithful assembly! We must all still have faith that what we ask for in Jesus' Name will still be granted to us! Remember, however, that we must accept God's answer, even if His answer is a "No"! Will you pray with me for all of our needy brothers and sisters gathered here tonight?"

There was agreement among the crowd!

With Rev. Smith's confidence strengthened, he continued, "If you have a need to bring before the Lord tonight, please step forward and present your petition."

Sam stood up and allowed Barb and Sara to go first, and then he followed. They were the first in line and as Barb began to explain Sara's illness to the pastor, Sam reached into his shirt and began to pull out an object.

Suddenly Sam was struck from two directions at once, as security tackled him. The object in his hand was flung toward the stage. When it landed on the floor in front of Rev. Smith the lid exploded off the plastic flask splattering whiskey all over his shoes. As the aroma of alcohol assaulted the pastor's nostrils, Barb and Sara looked down at Sam with hurt, embarrassment and fear in their eyes. As the two security officers lifted Sam from the floor and dragged him before Rev. Smith, tears could be seen running down his face.

Rev. Smith was about to shout angrily at Sam when Sara pulled on the Rev. Smith's pants leg and said through her own tears, "Don't hurt my daddy, he's sick! Please help him! That's why I brought him here! I want my parents to be happy when I die and I don't want Daddy getting sick and hitting my mommy when I'm gone. I know Jesus can help him because he told me to get them here and He would help them!"

Rev. Smith looked down at Sara through his own tears, which had begun to flood onto his cheeks, and said, "No one's going to hurt your daddy, honey. We thought he had a gun or some other harmful weapon."

He looked at Sam and said, much more irritably than he intended to, "What do you have to say for yourself, Sam?"

Sam looked up and said through his sobs, "I was supposed to kill you, Pastor. I owe a gambling debt and they said I must pay or kill you. If I don't, they will kill my little Sara." Sam wiped his eyes and nose on his sleeve and continued, "I just couldn't do it. If you check our tent you'll find a plastic gun under my pillow."

Rev. Smith nodded at security and one of the officers left to do just that.

Sam looked into Rev. Smith's face and said, "I was

trying to hand you the flask, so that I could publicly admit that I'm an alcoholic and ask your God to take my worthless life instead of my sweet Sara's for I deserve to die! I'm already damned to Hell for my actions, but Sara has her whole sweet life ahead of her."

As security released him, both Sara and Barb ran up and hugged Sam.

Rev. Smith watched them for a moment. Looking out over the crowd, he noticed the flood of emotions that filled the hearts of the believers and spilled over into their expressions of compassion.

He then said to the crowd, "With faith like this, can we do less than to pray that their requests be granted. Let's join together and pray that Sam's alcoholism be cured and that he'll never desire another drink, ever! I think we can help Sam with his debt, as well, but he'll need to promise never to gamble again and for that he'll, again, need God's help. Let's also pray that Sara be cured of her..."

He turned to Barb with the unasked question of what's wrong with Sara.

Barb said, as she handed the pastor the medical test results, "She has a cancerous brain tumor and we want Jesus to heal her."

Rev. Smith had a thought and said, "Let me remind all of you of what Josh said at every meeting that I've attended. He said that Jesus loves each and every one of us and has the power to save our souls and heal our bodies. Of this there can be no doubt! What we need to remember, however, is that we must pray in God's will! We may not understand God's Will or even agree with it, but we must obey it! Josh has always reminded us that if we pray for healing and don't get it, that we either have something in our lives that we must correct before the healing can occur or we need to ask again, persistently and finally we must accept the fact that the answer from Jesus is simply, "No". We don't always understand the "No" answer, but we will some day. In the mean time, let's pray in faith as we keep these things in our hearts!"

Rev. Smith, the many ministers and the crowd of Christians all prayed for the healing of Sam, Sara and the many others who'd come to petition their God. Many were cured instantly; Sam among them, while some were partially cured and others weren't cured at all. Sara, as later medical tests would show, was among the latter group. As a matter of fact, the tumor was growing at a much faster rate than before!

*　　*　　*

Josh was running after the light but couldn't quite enter it.

When he'd stop to rest, Jesus would appear to him and say, "Don't stop now, Josh, the race has just begun!"

The Lord would then dissolve and Josh would renew his efforts to enter the light, which always managed to stay just out of his reach. As he ran, the floor suddenly opened beneath his feet and he felt himself falling. He sensed rather than saw the ground racing up to meet him. Just when he knew that he would be smashed by the impact of his body against the ground, he jumped and was suddenly wide awake.

He tried to move but couldn't. He opened his eyes but there was only total darkness. He strained to hear, something, anything, but there was only silence. When Josh tried to shout, he found his mouth was taped shut. His ears throbbed with the sound of his own heart pounding in his chest, as his heart sped up to match the growing fear that was creeping into his soul. Tape or no, Josh screamed as he felt the cold, evil presence of a demonic being enter the room and felt it in his soul.

Tumult laughed as he watched the struggling, fearful, man of God.

Sweat beaded on Josh's forehead and his eyes were wide with fear as the gut wrenching panic threatened to drive him mad. Then suddenly, something began to tug at the back of Josh's brain just out of his reach and he grabbed for it desperately.

Tumult said with a smile, "Joshua White! First you'll suffer, then you'll die and this time you'll not rise!"

Tumult gave a hand signal and the small demon's of fear, despair and hopelessness slithered onto Josh's helpless body digging their knurled claws into his heart and brain laughing with glee as Josh continued to scream.

Joshua reached deep into his soul and remembered the way Jesus had always taken care of him. He ignored his fear, whispering, "In the name of Jesus be gone, Demons of fear, despair, hopelessness and anger."

The three demons screamed in unison and puffed out of existence.

Josh's body became weaker as they fought but his spirit was washed and strengthened with the Grace of God. His fear began to subside and Josh realized that he was in for the spiritual battle of his life.

Tumult straddled Josh's squirming body and clawed at his tortured soul. Josh continued to fight for his life and while doing so the confidence in his Lord grew with every attack. He knew that nothing could separate him from his Lord; Jesus Christ.

CHAPTER NINE

GRANNY INTERPRETS
JOSH'S DREAM

Vice President, Phillip Huggens, popped a couple of antacids into his mouth; he was terrified and if his ulcers were any indication, his nervous system was approaching meltdown. Huggens stood before the large oak doors, straightened his tie and wiped the top of his shoes on the back of his suit pants, as if shiny shoes would help him with the committee. He'd never met with the committee before. All of his orders were on prerecorded messages sent to him over secured phone lines. His father had convinced him that the committee was real and that it had been in existence since before the founding of this country. Huggens' father had also taught him that the committee was made up of the twelve most powerful and wealthy men and women in the world. People on the committee today had to be direct descendants of its original founders. Each person came from a different country and considered him or herself a protector of the world's interests. People couldn't rise to power, either politically or in private enterprise, without the committee's approval and seldom did anyone get asked into their actual presence. Huggens wasn't sure, therefore, if he'd been invited here on business of extreme importance or if they just wanted to witness his execution personally.

He raised a shaky fist, rapped timidly on one of the double doors and jumped out of his skin when both doors began to open smoothly inward on their silent mechanical hinges.

The leader of the committee watched as the nervous, shaky Huggens stumbled into the dark room. The only light in the room was focused on a small chair located in the middle of the room about five feet below the committee's raised platform. The platform contained twelve closed circuit transmitter/receiver monitors. None of the committee ever came in person that would be far too dangerous and time consuming. They could hear and speak as if they were present and the extremely bright flood lights at their "feet" guaranteed their visitors wouldn't catch on to their absence. This system had saved their lives more than once when some misguided, suicidal soul had tried to assassinate the entire committee, all at one time. Their survival of these attempts had allowed their reputation to grow to supernatural proportions and now their reign of terror had gone unopposed for years. Huggens raised his right hand in an attempt to shield his eyes.

"Sit down Mr. Huggens!" an amplified voice thundered.

The leader smiled when Huggens, who had just begun his descent into the chair, jumped up and then hurriedly sat back down again almost missing the chair in his attempt. The leader enjoyed how his voice boomed through the elaborate equipment making it sound grand and quite terrifying. It always struck fear into the very bones of his guests, which brought joy to the hearts of the committee members.

The leader's thoughts were interrupted, when Huggens dared to speak, "W-What can I do for you?"

The leader pushed the speaker button and angrily yelled, "We'll do the talking, Mr. Huggens, and you'll listen! Is that understood?"

The leader and most of the people on the committee had to suppress their laughter as the color drained from Huggens' face.

"Furthermore, Mr. Huggens, you'll carry out our wishes without fail, is that understood?"

"Y-Yes!"

"Yes what!"

"Y-Yes Sir!"

The leader was pleased. They'd picked the right man for the job. He'd do anything they told him to do, if he didn't have a heart attack first, they could also count on Huggens' fear of them to overcome his fear of the assignment they were about to give him.

*   *   *

President Roberta Place was sitting in front of her fireplace pretending to read some reports, when in fact she was watching her nine-year-old son, Patrick, playing chess with his computer. Roberta marveled at his skill. She glanced back at her reports. She'd been reviewing the progress she'd made thus far. Things had gone quite well actually, in the two short years since she'd witnessed the unearthly battle between Tumult and his horde of demons and Worl, Joshua White and their Christian army. A battle which had come to be known as the Battle of Covenant and had begun a revival in the United States

83

bringing more citizens to Jesus Christ than ever before.

With the help of mountains of mail from Christians all over the world and the nudging of the Holy Spirit, the Supreme Court Justices had finally agreed to reconsider the mistakes of the past and had finally met with Joshua White and the President. Joshua had strong arguments and explained the experiences he'd had in heaven. He shared a message from the Lord Jesus to the United Stated leaders and then he'd persuaded them to pray with him. It was a glorious sight!

Now, after a month of "closed door" meetings, the Supreme Court of the United States of America had reversed its position on Roe vs. Wade, prayer in public schools and governmental meetings, and many more issues where a public show of faith had been prohibited. They'd also agreed to talk to her about the possibility of reducing their United Nations involvement, if she could get Josh to come back to Washington to discuss it with them. She was really beginning to feel that success had finally arrived but it wasn't without cost. She was being blasted in the liberal media as a religious fanatic and they'd sworn to beat her in next month's election.

"Was it next month already", she thought.

This had been a short four years. Besides pushing these changes through the high levels of government, she'd also campaigned during the last year at a breakneck pace, in her bid for re-election.

Roberta thought, *"At least my ratings are still high in the poles and I still have a good chance!"*

Her only weak spot had been Huggens. He had fought her all the way forcing her to announce a change of running mates, which she was afraid, would hurt her election chances. It had been the right thing to do, however, both morally and apparently politically. As soon as she publicly dumped Huggens, her ratings rose. When she announced the conservative and very popular, Senator Thomas Holstrum from Texas, as her new running mate, their ratings soared to unheard of heights!

She found that she liked Tom. He was easy going, intelligent and still had a sense of humor, which was something lacking around the White House for years. She was looking forward to working with him on the many projects still left unfinished and they agreed on the solutions they wanted to bring about.

Roberta jumped slightly when the phone rang, which reminded her that her nerves were on edge despite the success. "Hello! Place speaking!"

"Good evening, Madam President."

Roberta slumped back into her chair and rolled her eyes, "Yes, Mr. Huggens, what can I do for you this evening?"

"Well, Madam President, I really need to come over and talk to you about some urgent business that has come up."

Roberta hated the way Huggens made everything seem like life and death, "Oh alright Mr. Huggens, come on over, but please make it brief!"

"Oh, I will, Madam President, I assure you!"

A chill ran down Roberta's spine as she hung up the phone. She turned to Patrick and said, "Would you take your game into your room, Patrick, Mr. Huggens and I need to talk business."

"OK mom."

He gave her a quick hug, and then walked carefully

to his room balancing the computerized chessboard as he went.

Roberta smiled as she listened to the insistent and somewhat, irritated sounding chess board, as it complained repeatedly, "Come on Patrick it's your move. I don't have all day you know!" Patrick mumbled back, "Shut up or I'll deactivate you and play video games instead."

Just then, there was a knock on the door.

Roberta whispered, "You didn't waste any time, did you Mr. Huggens?"

She opened the door, forced a smile and said, "Come on in, Phillip, how are you this evening?"

A very nervous, fidgeting Huggens said, "I-I'm fine Madam President."

He just stood there looking lost, so Roberta asked, "Well what's this pressing business you spoke of Phillip?"

"Well, Madam President..."

"Phillip, can you at least cut this Madam President business when we're alone? Just call me Roberta!"

"Well, Roberta, I heard you were sick and I..."

"You heard I'm sick? I'm not sick Huggens!"

"I also heard that you want me to take over for awhile."

Roberta was confused, "I want you to take over? I don't want you to take over Huggens! What's this nonsense?"

Huggens pulled a tape recorder out of his pocket and said, "I'm sorry for the deception, Roberta, but I had to get you on tape ordering me to take over for awhile. You did bring this on yourself, you know! Did you really think they'd leave you in office with all the damage you've already done? I think not!"

Huggens had developed an evil sneer, along with a new confidence, that had been lacking only seconds before. Suddenly, the shadows moved, and Roberta felt the sting of a needle just before the darkness overcame her.

*   *   *

It was 11:00 P.M. before Rev. Smith, Grady and Ellen were alone in the tent. They had witnessed many miracles and heard many testimonies about God's love and generosity this evening, but nothing seemed able to rid them of the cloud of doom and dismay which hung over them, not even the glory that God had shown them this evening. The subject had inevitably come back to Josh and his whereabouts. To ease the pain which that subject brought, Ellen had told Rev. Smith and Grady about the recurring vision that Josh had been having.

Ellen finished by saying, "What do you think it means Pastor?"

Rev. Smith was disturbed by the dream, and he asked Ellen, "Why didn't Josh tell Granny Girard about this dream earlier?"

Ellen shrugged her shoulders and said, "I don't know, Pastor, except that he was too worried about helping the people who were flocking to him daily for help. He just didn't take the time to visit Granny. He did, however, yell to me to make sure that we told Granny. Maybe we should do that first thing in the morning?"

Suddenly, the tent flap was thrown open and a young man entered carrying Granny Girard in his arms.

Granny's familiar, raspy voice spoke almost in a whisper, as if she were describing events unfolding before her very eyes saying, "The dark cloud is the sin of the Americans turning from their God. The quicksand is the punishment of death, which comes when a nation cuts itself off from the vine of Jesus Christ. The White House represents President Place's act of repentance and her subsequent efforts to right the wrongs done. Our country has begun to turn back to the ways of our God and to accept Jesus as His Son.

The dark figure in the dream is a demon Captain, named Tumult, who it appears, has returned to strike down President Place in order to throw the country under judgment again. Joshua, with the help of angelic forces, will have to face this foe, yet again, and may have already faced him. I think that President Place is in danger, but don't you go and waste any more time praying for her or Joshua! Don't you know that they are already in God's hands? You'll do better if you pray for their enemies as God taught you to do! That'll heap hot coals upon their heads!

Now, if you'll excuse me, this young man and I have an appointment to keep!"

Rev. Smith was stunned by Granny's sudden announcement and then departure. In a split second he thought about the fact that this woman, who though over a century old, still came to church every Sunday with one family or another...everyone in Rev. Smith's church took turns picking her up. Two Sundays ago, however, was her last. The Johnson's were wheeling her up the ramp of a local restaurant after the service, when Mr. Johnson suddenly grabbed his chest and fell. The chair traveled down the ramp backward and tipped over at the bottom-spilling Granny onto the ground breaking her hip in three places.

Mrs. Johnson had stopped by the hospital room later that day to apologize for the accident, but Granny just smiled her purest most humorous smile and said, "Are you kiddin! That's the most excitement I've had in years!"

The two women laughed and cried, and in general supported each other. It turned out that Mr. Johnson's heart attack had been a mild one, but Granny's broken hip would take a few months to heal if it healed at all.

Rev. Smith knew that Granny was stubborn and tough, but he didn't think she should be out this late and he yelled, "Granny, wait a minute, you shouldn't be out on a chilly night like this!"

They could hear Granny cackle as the tent flap closed.

Rev. Smith yelled, "Wait Granny, We'll take you back..."

By this time Grady and Rev. Smith had gone through the flap, they looked both ways and saw...no one!

A chill ran down their spines! They immediately returned to Ellen and explained that Granny had been too fast for them. They still didn't understand how she could have done it. The three of them joined hands and dutifully, but much less than happily, began to pray for their enemies as Granny had instructed them.

CHAPTER TEN

THE WARNING

Spike had very impatiently waited two days for verification that the one million dollars had been transferred to his Swiss account. Winter, Spike's second in command, had proven himself to be very faithful over the years. Therefore, Spike had trusted Winter to retrieve the expense money and bring it back to him. When Winter arrived back in the camp, he handed Spike an envelope containing the two hundred thousand dollars of expense money that he'd picked up at the secret drop point and told Spike that the transfer to the Swiss account was now complete.

Spike took half the money out of the envelope and handed it to Winter saying, "Pay the men."

Each would get paid according to rank and years of service. It was all very fair and civilized for such a ruthless gang of men.

Spike then continued his instructions, "Prepare to move out at dawn."

That had been several hours ago. Presently, however, Spike was sitting knee to knee with Sister Gen at her kitchen table. He was looking into her beautiful green eyes that always reminded him of cat's eyes, which is why he'd nicknamed her Catty. Their fingertips caressed the slide of Catty's Ouija Board. Catty had long, thin and somewhat, pale fingers with long, well manicured nails. Spike felt a presence about her. A force that he couldn't identify other than it always made him a bit nervous. He'd never admit to this nervousness, of course, but it was there nonetheless.

As was their practice on important occasions like this, they asked the Ouija Board many questions about the upcoming mission to Covenant. Spike was getting bored, however, and peeked at his watch noticing that it was 11:15 P.M. already. He decided that they could be spending this time in much more pleasant ways and was about to suggest it when Catty said, "Great Spirit Guide tell us true, will Spike be successful in this mission for you?"

Spike watched in fascination as the slide began to move toward the "yes" that was printed on the board. Suddenly, the slide flew across the room and slammed against the far wall of the trailer. The lights began to flicker on and off. Catty and Spike screamed as excruciating pain assaulted their nervous systems. The Ouija Board suddenly caught on fire and burned their hands. They both jumped to their feet knocking over their chairs, the table and the board.

The trailer lights stabilized and after a quick inspection Spike found no serious burns on either of their hands. Just then Catty inhaled loudly and a low inhuman growl rumbled from her throat. Catty's alabaster skin turned even paler than usual, and her eyes became dark, sunken orbs with a red glow. Thick, dark blue veins suddenly boiled, bulged and pulsated on Catty's face and forehead as she spoke in an eerie, deep, male voice.

It said, "Jarrett White! Beware of Covenant! Do not take on this job, for death awaits you in Covenant! Death to everything that you are and stand for! Seek instead the pleasures of this woman and wait for another job to come, for there will be many more!"

A cold, otherworldly wind ripped through the trailer knocking over shelves and spilling their contents onto the floor. The wind was replete with the disembodied screams of the damned. It was more than the two disciples of Satan could take. Catty screamed, collapsed onto her hands and knees and began to vomit dark green bile from the depths of her stomach. The stench caused Spike's own stomach to rebel forcing him to escape to the freshness of the night air.

As he reached for the door, Spike said with a voice that dripped with contempt, "I'll see you outside as soon as you finish fouling your trailer floor!"

Spike turned the knob of the door but nothing happened. The door was held fast by an unseen force and would not open. The wind became fierce and fear forced bile into Spike's throat causing it to burn.

Catty looked up at him, her eyes glowing red and she sprayed his pant legs with bile, as the disembodied voice screamed frantically, "Remember! Stay away from Covenant or pay the consequences!"

Spike had been frantically pushing on the door, panic threatening to drive him mad. Suddenly, it was allowed to open and he stumbled out into the night. The door slammed angrily behind him.

The evening breeze was chilly but inviting and it helped Spike to fight off his own nausea and dizziness.

Spike took a deep breath then looked up from the task of buttoning his jacket against the chilly night air. He dug a joint out of his pocket and noticed, to his disgust, that his hands were shaking slightly as he lit it.

He took a long drag and held the powerful drug in his lungs as long as he could then exhaled.

Just as the drug began to soothe Spike's shattered nerves, he noticed the crowd of people who'd come running, with weapons drawn, when they heard the commotion coming from Sister Gen's trailer.

As Catty stumbled weakly from the trailer the crowd stared with their mouths agape. Sister Gen's face still looked sinister, even though she'd put on clean jeans and shirt she still looked rough. She was trying to button her own jean jacket but her hands shook too badly so she opted for the joint in Spike's hand instead. She took a long drag and held it while Spike buttoned her jacket for her. Catty handed the joint back to him, reached into the pockets of her jacket and pulled a can of beer from each. She handed one to Spike then opened her own and gulped about half of it without taking a breath.

The crowd was whispering about Sister Gen's appearance; her face still pulsated with those hideous, demonic veins! Some even swore that her eyes were glowing red or was it just reflected firelight?

Before they could decide, Spike glared at the people and yelled, "Do you mind? We'd like a little privacy here!"

Knowing they'd get no explanation and being too afraid of Spike to ask for one, everyone simply turned around and went back to his or her own home, speculating on this strange occurrence. Spike and Catty each consumed about half a can of beer and finished the joint before they attempted to talk about their nightmarish experience.

Catty finally forced words out of her constricted throat and gasped; "I've never felt Aliron so afraid."

Spike asked, "Aliron? Oh yes! He's your Spirit Guide, right?"

"Yes, he is very afraid of something! He's never taken me over so forcefully before and he'd never make me sick like that unless he really was afraid for your safety. Spike, you must listen to his warning and stay away from Covenant! There's more danger there than you'd ever imagine!"

Spike smiled at Catty's sincere concern. Saying, as gently as he was able, "Well, I'm very flattered that you and ugh, this Aliron character, care so much for my safety and all; but I've taken the job, I've been paid, so I must go!"

Spike belched, squeezed his can flat and threw it on the desert floor. He put his arm around Catty's waist and led her toward her trailer.

Then, remembering the stench, he stopped and turning her around said, "We'll spend the night in my trailer Catty." She didn't resist; she didn't want to re-enter her trailer anyway. She, as well, didn't want to spend the night alone, but rather longed for the warmth and strength of Spike's body against hers.

For the first time since she'd begun sharing Spike's bed, they held each other in mutual support and compassion, which they both so badly needed. They were free of their usual lust, and suddenly felt very peaceful both slipping easily into a deep sleep.

*   *   *

Aliron, Catty's demon, was sweating and reeked of fear as he cowered in the corner of Spike's home eyeing the angelic warriors who surrounded him.

He and Boliczar, Spike's demon, had been having fun manipulating these humans. They liked nothing better than the Ouija board; it allowed them to give the humans all manner of false information. Sure there was always a grain of truth in what they had to say, for realism; but the information was usually slanted just enough to make the information false. It did, however, allow them to gain the complete trust of the humans who would then, very stupidly, invite them into their bodies for a visit. That's when the demon's fun would really begin!

Both demons had taken turns moving the slide across the board and they'd enjoyed laughing at the human's reactions, as well as, their gullibility.

The woman had just asked, "Great Spirit Guide tell us true will Spike be successful in his mission for you?"

Aliron shrugged his shoulders, as he started to place his finger on the pointer and said to Boliczar, "I think I'll say yes this time."

They were laughing as the slide began to move across the board. It was then, that Aliron felt the first slight tremor and heard the distant roar, which was quickly closing in on them.

He threw the slide across the room in his panic and in an attempt to get Catty's attention Aliron set the board on fire as he yelled to Boliczar, "Hide! Hide now! It's upon us!"

Aliron then quickly vaporized and slipped into Catty's body.

Boliczar asked, "What's upon us? I don't..."

When the shock wave hit Boliczar, he exploded in a puff of foul smelling, sulfuric smoke.

Aliron watched his partner "die", as he thought, *"It just can't be! No one has prayed for their enemies in... in... well in a very long time! I thought we had rid humans of that notion once and for all, but here it is. These Christians must never know what a powerful weapon they have. If they do, we're doomed! The power they'll generate will totally devastate our demonic forces!"*

His inner demon sense centered the disturbance around Covenant.

His fear mounted as he thought, *"I must stop these people before they lead me into that stronghold!"*

Aliron roughly took total possession of Catty and spoke a warning that he hoped would save his own neck, "Jarrett White! Beware of Covenant..."

After the humans had slipped outside to get high, Aliron had relaxed just a little and thought that most of the danger was passed. He was still in total possession of Sister Gen, of course, but something was tickling the fur on the back of his neck.

Once the humans had returned to Spike's trailer and had entered the bedroom, Aliron settled down for a peaceful night.

Suddenly, the warm peaceful hiding place of Sister Gen's soul, in which Aliron hunkered, exploded when an angelic hand grabbed Aliron by the scruff of the neck and pulled him roughly out of Sister Gen's body. He found himself dangling eyeball to eyeball with the mighty Capt. Worl and he didn't miss the two guards, who were always present on Worl's left and right, known by the same names.

Worl smiled at Aliron and said, "It would be in your best interest to leave, wouldn't you agree?"

Worl then threw Aliron into the corner of Spike's bedroom where he cowered while trying to balance what Worl would do to him if he stayed, with what Tumult would do if he left. In the end, he found it was best to escape the immediate danger and try to avoid Tumult's wrath later.

As soon as Worl had pulled Aliron from Sister Gen's restless body, her features had returned to normal and both humans slept innocently and peacefully together in Spike's bed.

Capt. Worl smiled at the couple and then left his ever present guards, Left and Right, to watch over them. These faithful guards were as large as Worl and had protected him for thousands of years, but just for tonight, they'd watch over these two humans. Humans, who still, out of ignorance, fought the very God who was trying to save them.

*   *   *

Tumult looked down at Joshua White's limp form with a new respect. He'd been fighting with him for hours now and with no angelic interference at all! The more time that passed the weaker Joshua's resistance became, although it had been more formidable than Tumult had expected.

Tumult was just about to try to possess Joshua, when Josh whispered, "Lord bless my captors with all of your blessings and fill them with Your Holy Spirit." Josh then passed out. A chill ran down Tumult's spine. He knew instinctively what it was and for the first time since Satan's torture chamber, his black heart was filled with real fear!

Tumult streaked from the room just as a blazing white sword swished past the right side of his neck. Aaron didn't hesitate, but streaked after Tumult. As they blazed across the night sky, Tumult's mind was reeling. If Aaron caught up with him while he had this much power, well, even Tumult wasn't sure of the outcome. Tumult could never figure out why Satan had agreed to this pact with God in the first place!

He thought, *"I suppose Satan had agreed that if any human would pray for good things to happen to the people who harmed them, powerful shock waves would reap havoc among the demon world and would in turn allow angels to help the lost souls for whom the Christians prayed. Satan never figured that God could actually get anyone to do it!"*

As Aaron sped ever closer to him, Tumult remembered the first time that they'd felt this powerful curse take hold. It was when Jesus, then only five years old, had prayed for God to forgive another boy who had hit him in the eye. Even as his eye turned black and swelled shut, he prayed for this boy's soul. That was the longest thirty minutes of Tumult's evil life, at least until now! Never did they foresee the damage that Jesus would do with this pact, while hanging on the cross or after his death, when he stormed the gates of hell, rising victorious over Satan, sin and death. Tumult had hoped that no one would ever discover this secret again, but here it was!

Tumult felt, rather than saw, the sword and was barely fast enough to repel Aaron's mighty blow. What followed was a frenzied thrashing, dodging and parrying of two mighty warriors, who were locked in the heat of battle. Their war cries rumbled across the night sky, as both warriors became weary. Just when Tumult thought that Aaron would get the upper hand, the accursed attack ended.

One second Aaron's sword was coming down on Tumult's head, the next split second, Aaron was gone, sword and all. The small group of Christians had stopped praying!

Tumult made contact with Crygen, his second in command and found that in the short fifteen minute span of time that had just transpired, they had lost over five-thousand of their demonic forces. Tumult held his sword over his head and screamed in rage!

Then with a sudden calm he said, as he put his sword back into it's sheath, "You Christians will pay for this! You'll all pay, but Joshua White will pay first! And he'll pay most dearly!"

*   *   *

Rev. Smith peeked at his watch and saw that it was 11:30. At Granny's insistence, they'd begun praying at 11:15, but he didn't feel that they were accomplishing anything. He didn't feel the peace, or the calm that he did when he prayed at other times.

He finally said to Grady and Ellen, "Look, let's stop for a minute, while I go and check on Granny. We don't even now who that young man was that was carrying her and I want to give that nursing home a piece of my mind; letting her out this late!"

By this time he'd reached the podium and picked up the phone book from behind it. He looked up the number for the Spring Air Rest Home, and dialed.

Grady and Ellen watched as he talked on the phone. "This is Rev. Smith. Oh I'm fine Joyce. Say, could you tell me who checked Granny Girard out this evening?"

As Rev. Smith listened, the color drained from his normally dark skinned face and he said, "Yes, thank you Joyce, I'll be in touch."

He put the phone down, and then faced Grady and Ellen, saying as he did so, "Granny Girard passed away at exactly 11:00pm this evening. Joyce had been talking to her when Granny smiled and said, 'Well Joyce, honey, my escort's here and I must be leaving you now. Take care of yourself and keep the faith alive in your heart.'"

"Joyce then said that Granny's eyes lost their focus and she said, 'Joyce, it is so beautiful, wait 'til you see it!'"

"With that, she simply stopped breathing and was gone. Do you realize that's the exact moment that she appeared to us here! That means..."

Grady exclaimed, "That the young man carrying Granny Girard was her Guardian Angel and they stopped here on their way to heaven to give us a message!"

Ellen said, "Then maybe we should...?"

Grady nodded agreement and held out his hands. Without a word Rev. Smith and Ellen each held one of Grady's hands and then each other's as they all resumed praying for their enemies. This time, however, they prayed with a renewed fervor that had been missing before.

*   *   *

The screams, death throes and excruciating suffering thrust upon the demons because of these prayers, would've driven the humans mad; if, of course, they could have heard them. As it was, they were totally oblivious to the damage they were causing to Tumult's troops or were they mindful of the plans that they were single-handedly thwarting.

Jesus watched with pleasure as his followers matured before his eyes.

CHAPTER ELEVEN
HOSPITAL OF THE DAMNED

It was a sparkling, brisk autumn morning. The birds were singing to their mates as Dr. Wilbur Kamerman, cup and saucer in hand, slid the double door of his dining room open and took a deep breath of fresh air. He took a sip of his tea, which contained cream and just a pinch of sugar. On the table next to him, there lay two folders marked "New Arrivals". The doctor, putting the folders under the arm that held the tea, opened the sliding screen door and stepped out onto his patio. He was instantly glad he'd worn his suit jacket, which gave him some protection from the chilly air; even so, it was an invigorating morning. The anticipation of new patients and the challenge that they represented had become one of the most exciting parts of the doctor's job and he always found a way to savor the moment. Dr. Kamerman walked up to the patio table, pulled out the chair and sat down with a satisfied sigh. The table's umbrella was neatly tied up and would, most likely, remain that way for the winter months to come. He propped his feet up on the adjoining chair, laid the files on the table and took cup and saucer in his left hand. As he removed the cup and took another satisfying sip of his morning tea he looked over the vast estate of which he was the ruler.

He often fantasized about himself as a king with all of his servants and loyal subjects. Yes, that was how he looked at his staff and patients!

"I'm in charge, after all!", he thought.

He prided himself on his accomplishments here at the hospital and marveled at how far he'd come. He had started here at the age of thirty; a young, idealistic psychiatrist. Now after thirty years of backstabbing and out maneuvering the competition, he was the Administrator and Senior Psychiatrist of the Blue Skies Veteran's Hospital!

He'd taken over about five years ago and loved it here. The day he took over, he moved into the massive mansion, which would belong to him as long as he held this position and he intended to hold this position just as long as he liked. He was also in charge of the secret CIA Mental Ward facility, located under his legitimate facility.

The table at which he sat was located behind his mansion and from this high ground Dr. Kamerman could look down on the Hospital, which was three stories tall. An asphalt golf cart trail led from his house to the hospital. He'd traveled this trail many times over the years sometimes walking, sometimes riding, basically depending upon his mood or the pressure of his duties.

As Dr. Kamerman looked around, he was astonished that the well-manicured lawn was still green and there were even some flowers still visible in the scattered flower gardens. The leaves had made their annual gradual color change and some had even begun to fall. The doctor realized, to his disappointment, that this would be the last breakfast that he'd enjoy on his patio until next spring. His reverie was interrupted when, to the doctor's left, a pair of Cardinals landed on the patio flapping and chirping happily. Then in a flutter of wings they were off again chasing each other from tree to tree.

The doctor thought about all of his "students", his

"special" patients, lodged in the secret wing. Many prominent people had passed through the doctor's "Special Program". Presidents of several countries, politicians, lawyers, doctors and many citizens who were important to the committee had occupied the doctor's **special guest rooms**". Dr. Kamerman, for his part, thought of the hospital as his own personal school of humanity to which people came disturbed and confused, but they left confident, sure and under the total control of the committee!

Dr. Kamerman chuckled to himself as he thought, *"The committee controlled the graduates, but he controlled the committee"*. As Chairman of the committee, Dr. Kamerman effectively ruled the world of politics and business without anyone suspecting his presence. Dr. Kamerman controlled everything from a special room in his secured "secret" facility. He'd always loved a good cloak and dagger mystery and had in fact, turned his life into one. He was the heir to millions of dollars and had no real money worries, so he had turned to the adventure of the mind. His family had chaired the Committee from its inception and had done so in secret, for at least two hundred years. Then five years ago when his father died, he'd assumed his father's duties and made his move on the past administrator of this facility who suddenly had a mysterious and fatal accident while away on a business trip. Dr. Kamerman had then moved all of his father's electronic equipment into a secret room and continued to contact and chair the committee as his father had before him, his grandfather before that and his great grandfather before that and so on. His slightest whim could be felt around the world in a matter of seconds. Yes, life was good and unbelievably kind to him!

Dr. Kamerman smiled as he sat his empty cup down and picked up the top folder.

He opened the cover and whispered, "Ah yes! Mr. Joshua White, we'll meet at last!"

He first looked at the photographs of which there were several. There was one of the young, "Special Forces" Joshua White and several more of Mr. White as a police officer. Even more were of White as he raised a mob against the proposed abortion clinic in Covenant. There were several of him at different times during the supposed Battle of Covenant, but none of the reported angels and demons showed up in the pictures.

"A pity!", thought the Doctor.

He also wondered what happened to the photographer who'd taken them. He'd sent the pictures, but then simply vanished.

"Curious", thought Dr. Kamerman.

A new photographer took the next series of pictures and they told the doctor a lot about White's current activity in Covenant. There were pictures of a line of cars, "several miles long", a hand written note said at the bottom of the picture. There were mobs of people filing into a tent in the middle of a field. More pictures showed White praying over vast crowds of people and others showed happy people turning in their crutches, wheelchairs and even people holding signs that read, "The Lord gave His answer, He cured me of my cancer!"

These pictures spoke volumes of information to Dr. Kamerman and he was going to enjoy breaking this

Joshua White. The Committee could certainly use White to turn these vast crowds to its own devices.

The photographers, which seemed to Dr. Kamerman to have defected to the enemy's side, gave Dr. Kamerman an uneasy feeling about this Sam Crawford he'd sent into Covenant to kill Rev. Smith. He shrugged his shoulders and thought, *"We might get lucky this time, but I won't hold my breath!"*

Next, the doctor opened a file marked "TOP SECRET" and pulled out a report which stated that Joshua White had been promoted out of the Special Forces into the elite "Cleansing Force" of the CIA. It had been a very short career. After two short months there was a hearing about the "Odd Behavior" of the new recruit, Joshua White. According to the report, which followed the events of the hearing, Joshua White, who'd served his country for almost two years with distinction, was now disobeying orders, refusing to go on certain missions and was becoming a national security risk.

In a statement prepared by White, himself, he stated, "I would never have joined the "Cleansing Force" had I known that their purpose was to kidnap and even kill innocent children, Presidents of other countries and anyone else who was deemed dangerous. We are not even told why they're the enemy of our country. This is a dangerous practice and flies in the face of all that I believe! Neither my moral character, nor my Christian faith, will allow me to carry out such obvious sins as attacking innocent children!"

The doctor whispered, "He's got guts, I'll give him that!"

He then read further and found that it was later

determined, that Joshua White was not mentally stable enough to continue his duties in this unit. He was given an honorable discharge from the force. He'd been sworn to secrecy and was even put under surveillance for three years. During that time, he'd reported in every three months for a lie detector test, to make certain that he hadn't told anyone about any of the operations. After that, the report showed they'd left him pretty well alone to live out a somewhat dull career in the **Covenant** police force. Dull, that is, until about two years ago.

Dr. Kamerman closed the file and thought about the Covenant incident. Governor Bradley, who besides being the warlock of the largest and most powerful Coven in his State, had also been one of Dr. Kamerman's best "students". Yes, Dr. Kamerman had personally programmed Governor Bradley for the task of making Christianity illegal. A plan that would've worked if not for the interference of Joshua White. They'd thrown everything at him, but to no avail. They'd tried to kill him, but he not only survived, he somehow killed over two hundred National Guard troops, General Frietegg and Governor Bradley. To add insult to injury, he somehow turned President Place into one of his puppets, undoing all of the doctor's hard work with her, as well. These thoughts didn't anger the doctor, for he enjoyed a good challenge and besides, they served to remind him just how dangerous this Joshua White could be. There would most assuredly have to be special precautions taken with him. He was also looking forward to breaking into White's mind and finding the secrets to his power. As much power as Dr. Kamerman had, he was always willing to increase his advantage over others.

As Dr. Kamerman put Joshua's file down, he noticed movement off to his right. He watched as Angela walked toward him carrying a tray. Angela was his favorite student. She'd come to him about a year or so ago, in a witness protection program. Instead of killing her as he'd done to others sent to him, which by the way saved the government millions in support dollars, he simply brainwashed her, programming her to serve his every need and desire. She'd served him very well indeed.

Lust filled his eyes as Angela put the tray on the table and poured him another cup of tea and then placed a plate of bacon, eggs, pancakes and two links of sausage in front of him. She buttered his pancakes, poured syrup on them, then bent over and kissed him on the lips. Without a word, she picked up the tray and turned to leave.

She paused, allowing Dr. Kamerman to pat her bottom and say, "I'll see you tonight Angela."

She smiled through her trance-like state and walked slowly back into the house. He had five other women serving him, but Angela was his favorite and his most successful accomplishment.

He sighed, "Life is good!"

He then turned his attention to the next file and read it as he ate his breakfast.

As he opened the file, he whispered through a mouth full of eggs, "Ah, Roberta Place, you're as beautiful as ever!"

He stared at her picture for a long while and as he ate he remembered all the fun he'd had humiliating her the last time she was here.

Roberta Place had been the first woman elected to

the Office of President. That was enough to make her a remarkable woman, but she had many other talents as well, that attracted the committee's attention. She was ruthless in her business, but had a good public image, a perfect balance and was a perfect politician; even though, she had the draw back of being a family woman. It'd been easy to arrange for her husband's murder, however, and even easier to arrange for her to be brought to this military hospital for a rest after the funeral.

During her "rest" here, Dr. Kamerman had been able to program her into trusting and even falling in love with Governor Bradley. The Committee wanted him in the public eye as her husband for a while to set the stage. If she turned on them or became a liability, he could then run for the office himself. Who would be able to resist voting for the husband of a murdered President? Another good plan ruined by Joshua White's interference!

Now, with Bradley dead and Place under Joshua's power, Dr. Kamerman had to start all over again, but he didn't mind a challenge. As a matter of fact, if truth be told, he thrived on the prospect.

Dr. Kamerman had finished his breakfast during this trip down memory lane and after finishing his second cup of tea, he dabbed his mouth with his napkin.

He then whispered, "Yes! I think it's about time to finally get to work on this infamous Joshua White. But first, I must pay my respects to the honorable President of these United States!"

With a chuckle he picked up the files, climbed into his golf cart and drove toward the hospital while whistling a happy tune.

*   *   *

President Roberta Place had been drugged, transported to a secret installation, deposited in a secret cell and then awakened in her present, awkward position. She wasn't in a really good mood!

When she'd awakened early this morning, she found herself stripped down to her underclothing with her feet and ankles attached securely to the ceiling of the cell. As if hanging upside-down wasn't painful enough, they'd pierced her skin with several needles in different areas of her body. From the needles ran wires, which completed a circuit timed to deliver a jolt of electricity through every needle, all at once, every five minutes, causing every muscle in her body to spasm and convulse painfully.

At first, her screams had pierced the morning air of the soundproof cell but now only a hoarse croak was all she could manage. With the first jolts her muscles would stop their spasms just before the next electrical event sent them reeling again. Now, however, they were in a constant state of spasm and the President's mind was beginning to blank out which was, of course, the entire purpose of this torturous exercise.

Roberta was also haunted by the feeling that this was all too familiar that she'd been through this once before, but "No!", she thought, *I'd remember something like this, wouldn't I?!"*

Just then, the door of her cell opened and she saw a familiar face enter the cell. She croaked a hoarse cry as another jolt sent her reeling.

The man said, "Good morning Madam President, I

hope your stay has been, shall we say, enlightening so far this morning!"

Then it all came flooding back to her! This man had done this to her before! He'd raped her helpless body and had stolen what was left of her mind. He'd programmed her to do his bidding. She even remembered him introducing her to Governor Bradley. It'd all been a lie! She'd been a puppet and worse, for this man!

Dr. Kamerman could see the hatred enter the eyes of the President and he said, "Ah, I see that you do remember! Good! Good! It's unfortunate that I have to undo all of my programming, but I have to restore your memory so I can erase it again. That's the nature of the beast."

Dr. Kamerman laughed an evil, lustful laugh and gave Roberta a look that caused her skin to crawl with disgust. She watched as the man gave a hand signal and her body began to descend toward the floor. She was going to scream more hatred at the doctor, but another electric current sent her body into, yet another, fit of spasms.

As the President lay helpless on the floor before the doctor, she watched in fearful anticipation of what she knew he'd do next, when the cell phone rang.

The doctor angrily answered, "What! I told you not to disturb me!"

As he listened, a smile formed on his thin lips, "In that case, I'll be right there!"

He hung up the phone and looked down at the President. He squatted down and gently wiped a tear from her cheek, saying, "I know you're going to be disappointed, my dear, but it seems that Joshua White is ready for the next step in his treatment as well. You'll just have to be patient. I will, however, return to satisfy your every desire!"

President Place had never felt such hatred for another human being before and when he laughed in her face, she could take it no longer. With all of the fluid she could produce, she spat in the doctor's face. He stopped laughing, shocked that anyone would ever dare do that. He then backhanded her across the right cheekbone. When she came to, the doctor was leaving and her body was rising toward the ceiling, once again. A smile of satisfaction appeared on the President's face, as another electric shock sent the rest of her body reeling.

*   *   *

The evil presence was gone when Joshua awoke, but his condition hadn't changed. No one had approached him at all and he was still in this maddening darkness. It was still silent, except for the pounding of his own heart, which he heard inside his ears and he was still immobile. He was about to fall into panic again, but he forced himself to think rationally.

He thought, *"Why is this happening, and who would do this?"*

It was as if flood gates opened up in his mind and he thought, *"That's it! The Cleansing Force! I knew I recognized those tactics during my abduction. And, this treatment is just what they warned us would happen if we became a prisoner of war!"* He'd also studied the methods that cults used **as** brainwashing techniques.

"Deprive the subject of food and water. Deprive him

of all of his senses and if you're in a hurry, use drugs.", Joshua thought, as another method occurred to him, *"dehumanize the subject by stripping him or her of clothing, withholding bathroom facilities and any number of other inhumanities. Add to this pain, humiliation and fear; and you have the tools needed to break down anyone's normal defenses. Sooner or later you'll have a disoriented and vulnerably empty brain, into which you can pour all the false information you'd ever desire and the subject will become your willing tool."*

These thoughts didn't come quite this clearly to Joshua's foggy mind, but he understood the principle enough to know that he was in trouble. He also began to remember what his training in the Special Forces had taught him.

"If they deny your senses, grab onto anything you can and anchor yourself to that reality."

All of his senses were blocked, except the sense of smell. Until about a half an hour ago, however, there'd been nothing to smell in this clinical environment, not until he'd had no choice but to foul himself. It had disgusted him at first, but now he clung to the odor, it being his only anchor to reality, and even that was slowly slipping from his clouded mind.

Suddenly, the fog seemed to clear, ever so slightly and a new thought crept into his mind.

It was Aaron's voice, *"Pray Joshua! Pray!"*

With that thought came the words, *"The Ninety-First Psalm!"*

Joshua couldn't remember the words, so he whispered what he could remember through his gag, "The Ninety-First Psalm, The Ninety-First Psalm!"

Then, just a little more fog cleared and he said, "He that dwelleth in the secret place of the most High..."

Then it was gone. Joshua's anxiety was building as he forced himself to remember the words of this familiar prayer.

Then another break through, "...shall abide under the shadow of the Almighty..."

Gone again, but he would not give up, "The Ninety-First Psalm, The..."

Another flash and it was becoming clearer and stronger, "...For he shall give his angels charge over thee, to keep thee in all thy ways. They shall bear thee up in *their* hands, lest thou dash thy foot against a stone. Thou shalt tread upon the lion and the adder: the young lion and the dragon shalt thou trample under foot. Because he hath set his love upon me, therefore will I deliver him: I will set him on high because he hath known my name. He shall call upon me, and I will answer him: I *will* be with him in trouble; I will deliver him, and honor him. With long life will I satisfy him, and shew him my salvation."

Joshua had shouted these last words just as loud as his gagged mouth would allow, as he'd struggled against his restraints until at last he lay back exhausted.

The guard who was monitoring Joshua's vital signs saw them shoot off of the scale, then bottom out and he mistakenly thought that Joshua had finally cracked. With a sense of satisfaction, the guard called Dr. Kamerman, who was in the President's cell.

*　　　*　　　*

Aaron was enraged as he entered Joshua's cell. The puny demon that Tumult had left behind was sitting on Josh's chest pumping confusion and fear into his mind and heart. Aaron drew his sword and before the sluggish ghoul could react, Aaron sliced him in half. There was a satisfactory puff of acrid smoke, and then Aaron touched Josh's shoulder and said, "Pray Joshua! Pray!"

Aaron watched as Josh struggled to regain control over his tortured mind and Aaron offered all the strength he was allowed. When Joshua finally lay back exhausted, but victorious, Aaron knew it was time to appear.

As Joshua layback enjoying his new clarity of mind, the room began to glow. He then felt the restraints fall away and someone was rubbing feeling back into his numb feet and arms. Joshua squinted into the gloom and finally saw the dim light that made up Aaron's form. "Is that you, Aaron?"

"Just lie back and rest my friend. You've been through quite an ordeal, but you passed with flying colors! Now be faithful and follow your Christ filled heart in the events to come. You must stand up for Jesus in this life, that's why you're here. Now eat this and be strong."

With that, Aaron helped Josh sit up and handed him a small loaf of warm bread and a very pleasant smelling hot drink, then disappeared.

Joshua was still sitting in the utter darkness of his cell, but his soul was lit with the light of Christ. He was wearing fresh, clean clothes and he felt as though he'd taken a shower, somehow. It was very refreshing. As he ate and drank the heavenly food, it filled him with a strength that he thought he'd lost forever. A smile crept onto his lips, as he enjoyed his meal and his soul rested in the loving arms of his Savior, Jesus.

CHAPTER TWELVE
ENCOUNTERS

After their strange encounter with Granny Girard and her angel, Grady, Ellen and the pastor prayed for Josh's abductors until 4:00 in the morning. Finally, exhausted and bewildered Rev. Smith offered to take Ellen home, while Grady left to pick Marla up at the airport.

The morning air was chilly and Grady looked up at the stars and the moon as he walked toward his car. Grady prayed that Josh would be all right and left it totally in God's hands. As he drove to the airport, he wondered if Marla might do a news story on Josh's abduction and, in doing so, get some information from someone as to his whereabouts. He'd also have her ask for massive prayers, nation wide, for Josh's captors. If what Granny said was true, this should give them a headache or heartburn; he didn't care which!

Grady was so engrossed in his thoughts, he didn't notice the black sedan, which had followed him all the way from Jesus Park and turned into the airport right behind him.

*   *   *

Spike looked back at the line of mobile homes and smiled. He was happy and ready for action; therefore, it was with a light heart that he raised his hand and waved them forward, like some wagon master of the old west. As he rode his own new motorcycle out of camp and headed into the desert, Spike pondered last night's events. The drugs and alcohol had blotted out the fear and anxiety of the frightening experience, but they'd left a sour stomach and pounding headache in their wake.

When Spike and Catty had walked into his trailer last night, he'd seen his "old lady" sitting on the couch. She'd bandaged the worst of the blisters on her neck but there was still a lot of red, raw skin showing. Spike told her to go and clean up Sister Gen's trailer, then to report to Winter. She'd be his "old lady" now!

She was about to protest, but saw Spike take out a knife. The blade swished open and as he flipped it over into the throwing position, she ran from the trailer tears running freely down her cheeks.

Spike had then told Catty, "Winter's had his eyes on her and she's looked back on occasion, so now they can both be happy!"

Catty smiled at Spike, knowing that she'd just been promoted to his main woman, a prospect that appealed to her very much! Spike respected Catty and was even getting fond of her, even though this worried him just a little.

Spike had decided to encamp just South of Covenant in the state park. While they were camped there, Spike would "scope out" the scene and make his plans. Spike thought again about the words Catty had spoken to him while using his real name. No one knew his real name and he hadn't even heard it himself for years. It was; therefore, a shock to be addressed that way twice in one week, once by that angelic creature and then again, by Catty's Spirit guide. The use of his real name had caused him to think of his home, his earlier identity and he wasn't at all comfortable with that!

Spike thought, *"It's too soon to take up my real identity..."*

A memory intruded on Spike's thoughts and he suddenly relived the argument that he and his father had about church and drugs. Jarrett had decided that drugs were more fun and much cooler than going to church. Church had become a place of fear and disgust, but he didn't want to think of that now! Jarrett also thought he knew much more than his father did about life, and wouldn't listen to his father's pleadings. Finally, he'd tired of hearing them at all and one day he just left town. He never said good-by and he never came back. For a while he had regrets and once he even thought that his father had been correct, but he soon buried those sentiments in the reality of life. He'd become reckless and then ruthless; he fared well in the Armed Services and later in the, well, in a secret organization. Then a little over two years ago he'd started his own gang. There'd been skirmishes with rival gangs over territory, etc., but Spike had decided to travel and the skirmishes diminished.

In just over two years, his reputation had spread throughout the underworld, as the best hit-man around. That was the start of a very lucrative business, which he'd conducted at the cost of many lives and broken dreams.

Spike whispered to himself, "What could Catty's Spirit Guide have meant by, the death of everything he was or stood for?" He put the uncomfortable question aside and tried to concentrate on the mission at hand, but as he raced toward Covenant a spirit of gloom overtook the Demon Slayer.

*   *   *

"Over here Marla!" Grady watched as Marla looked around, then spotting him began to jump up and down and wave. As they ran toward each other, Grady drank in the beauty of Marla Brinkle, News Anchor Woman. Marla's smile accented the green skirt and white silk blouse that she wore. Her eyes sparkled with the same sheen as her pearl necklace and matching earrings. Marla jumped into Grady's arms, he spun her around, they laughed, teased and thoroughly enjoyed themselves.

People stopped to stare at Grady, who still wore his Chief's uniform; they very seldom saw a police Chief happy and acting like a normal person! Grady ignored the gawking crowd as he took a deep whiff of Marla's intoxicating perfume while enjoying the warmth of their embrace. After they'd indulged themselves with a rather long kiss, they pulled back and just smiled into each other's eyes.

It had been the longest two weeks of Grady's life and he was glad that Marla was finally home! He knew that as a newsperson, Marla would always have trips to take and stories to follow, but he would never get used to it!

Grady smiled and even chuckled.

Marla laughed back, "What? What's so funny, Grady?"

Grady hugged Marla and said, "I was just thinking

about how I hated your guts just two years ago, but it seems a lifetime has passed since then!"

Marla teased as she wiped lipstick from Grady's lips, "You never told me you hated my guts, Grady!"

Grady blushed, "You know what I mean! There you were, this cold reporter who hated Christians and God even more, I think. You were undermining everything we stood for, then suddenly, we are thrown together into a situation where our love was forced to the surface, despite our best efforts to hide it, even from ourselves!"

Marla continued for Grady, "Yes, and I, for one, am glad that we've found each other! Any regrets Grady O'Leary?"

"Not a one, my love!"

They laughed and started walking toward the baggage claim area.

As they walked, Marla asked, "Any leads yet on Josh's abductors?"

Grady stopped, "How did you hear about that already?"

Marla gave him her sly smile and said, "I'm a reporter you know, but it's out on all the wires. Is Ellen all right?"

Grady became a little more serious, "Yes, she's holding up well and wasn't hurt too bad, physically, but the not knowing where or even why, they've taken Josh is going to wear on her."

Marla squeezed Grady's hand, "Yes, it would be awful! I just don't know what I'd do if it were you, Grady!"

Grady said, as he grabbed Marla's baggage, "Oh, by the way, let me tell you about the strange encounter that

Rev. Smith, Ellen and I had with Granny Girard and what we believe to be her guardian angel! We were in the tent last night after the service..."

As Grady told Marla about the angelic encounter, two men dressed in black suits raised the hood of Grady's squad car. They attached and activated a bomb and then gently lowered the hood. The men laughed as they walked slowly back to their own car to await the magnificent blast.

*   *   *

Dr. Kamerman was excited! He was finally going to meet the man who'd caused him so much trouble. For the last two years he'd heard all about the powerful Joshua White and how slippery he'd been as he, single-handedly, foiled all of their plans. Now, however, he lay in one of Dr. Kamerman's cells, a broken, mindless man. The doctor was confident that he could take Joshua's broken mind and heal it of all its mental delusions.

"After getting all of his secrets first, of course!", the doctor thought, as the attendant opened the door, then stood back.

It was a confident Dr. Kamerman who entered the cell. Just as the attendant switched the lights on, the doctor stopped short and gasped. Not only was Joshua White not the mindless, blank, broken man that Dr. Kamerman had expected, but also he was neither bound, nor gagged! In fact, he sat on his bunk, his legs crossed, eating the last of what looked like a steaming loaf of homemade bread and sipping on a cup of, who knows what!

Joshua looked at the doctor and said, "Come in, Dr. Kamerman, I've been expecting you."

The doctor fainted dead away and was hurriedly dragged from the cell by the bewildered attendant, who quickly slammed and locked the door behind them!

It was a contented Joshua, who asked with a smile, "Was it something I said?"

*   *   *

The two men in the black sedan, watched as Grady and Marla made their way toward Grady's car.

The happy couple laughed and talked as Grady opened the trunk and put Marla's bags away. Grady then unlocked the passenger door for Marla, teasing her that he should make her ride in the back so everyone would think he had a prisoner. She declined the offer, however, so after closing her door, Grady walked around to his side of the car.

He hesitated for a moment at the hood, thinking that something was out of place and the two men in the nearby sedan held their breath.

Grady, however, only reached down and wiped a smudge from the hood, shrugged his shoulders, and then got into his side of the car.

The two men sat forward but ducked low in case flying debris came their way. They waited what seemed like an eternity and then they heard...Grady's car start? This couldn't be! He was backing out; and now, they were getting away!

The passenger of the black sedan pulled out a remote detonator, saying, "Go after them, Leon!"

As he yelled the order, he pushed the button on the back up detonator, but again, nothing happened to Grady's car.

He roared, as he frantically pushed the button over and over, "This can't be! It should've blown his car and this backup has never failed, until now, that is!"

It was at this point, he noticed, they hadn't begun to move yet.

He bellowed, "Leon! What are you waiting for?"

Leon turned and hollered back, "It won't start, Andy, just like your generic bomb won't blow!"

Andy let out a stream of curse words that would've soured a sailor's beer, and shouted, "All right then! We'll just get another car! Let's go! We can't afford to lose them!"

*　　*　　*

Joshua was sitting on the edge of his bed rocking back and forth, he hadn't expected such a priceless reaction from the "good" doctor! The look on the man's face, when Josh said his name. . .

"Wow! If I'd just had a camera at that moment!", Joshua laughed.

Aaron had only told him that a Dr. Kamerman would be in soon and that was it. It had been enough!

The poor doctor was only 5'5" tall, about ninety pounds soaking wet, had a long pointed chin, beak-like nose and his high forehead spoke of much missing hair. He was wearing a gray suit, white shirt and red bow tie! If that hadn't been funny enough, the expression that had frozen on the doctor's face and his enlarged eyes made it hilarious! They'd forgotten to shut off the light, so Joshua just laid back and enjoyed the light praising God who'd come through for him, yet again. A God who apparently has a great sense of humor!

*   *   *

Grady was really enjoying Marla's company, as he pulled out of the Airport parking lot and onto the expressway. As they talked and caught up with each other's stories, the subject of their wedding came up, again. They'd just decided to really discuss it seriously, when there was a "pop" under the hood and the engine of Grady's squad car died. They'd just gone over the crest of a hill, so Grady coasted to a stop well off of the road so as to prevent someone from colliding with the rear of his car.

*   *   *

Jacob and Margerie Sparks left the terminal and walked to the familiar spot where they always parked their car. They'd just gotten back from a week in Florida and were looking forward to a peaceful drive home, then maybe a hot bath and some sleep.

As they approached lot 36A, Margerie punched Jacob and said, "Hey Jacob, that looks like our car!"

Sure enough, the two bewildered travelers had gotten home just in time to helplessly watch their stolen car being driven off without them.

*   *   *

127

Andy and Leon had found a suitable replacement for their broken down sedan and sped off after Grady's car. It had only taken a couple of minutes for these professionals to catch up with Grady and Marla, who weren't in any real hurry anyway.

When he caught sight of them, Andy pulled out another remote, pushed it's button and said, "I always have a backup plan, Leon. This button will disable his motor and he'll have to pull over! Then..."

As he said this, he pulled out his .357 Magnum and checked to be sure it was fully loaded.

*　　*　　*

As Grady looked under the hood, he scratched his head; he knew nothing about cars or how to make them run.

As he stood, staring at the engine, as if that would fix it, someone said, "Hey thar officer! Fur five bucks I'll fix that thar car fur ya."

Grady turned, he saw an old man walking toward him. The man wore old, dirty clothes, which looked as though they hadn't been washed for a while. He had gray hair, a couple of days growth of beard and he was chewing tobacco. Grady felt sorry for the man and figured it couldn't hurt anything.

He said, "Sure, give it a try, I'm afraid I don't know how."

Grady had already decided to give the man ten bucks, whether he fixed the car or not!

*　　*　　*

Andy rolled the window down on the passenger side and got ready to shoot. Grady's car had just disappeared below the crest of the hill, so he knew he'd have to shoot fast, and then get away. When they crested the hill, however, they saw Grady's car all right, but he wasn't alone. There was a wrecker in front of his squad car and another police car was behind it. Andy hurriedly put his gun down and told Leon to drive on past.

*   *   *

The man spit out his tobacco, wiped his mouth on a large blue bandanna, and said, "Well sonny, this har shouldn't be too much bother at tall! Just git in and giv'er a try."

A skeptical Grady slid behind the wheel, turned the key and the car started right up! He turned to Marla and said, "He really did it! The old man fixed it!"

Grady then got out, walked around the front of the car to thank the man; but when he cleared the raised hood, the man was nowhere to be found. Grady looked under the car, he looked both ways down the street, but he saw no one.

He closed the hood, got back into the car and asked, "Marla did you see where the old man went?"

She looked around and said, "No, I thought he was up front with you, that is, until you closed the hood and were standing there alone."

Grady started to pull out into traffic and as he looked to his left, he noticed a sedan passing him. He caught just the glimpse of what looked like a gun being slipped just out of sight.

Just then Grady's radio jumped to life and Mandy's familiar voice announced, "All units! Be on the lookout for a blue sedan, two male occupants, license number 3485284, stolen from the airport, just fifteen minutes ago!"

Grady looked at the car that had just passed them, then he looked over at Marla and said, "Can you believe this?"

As he said this, he pointed at the car in front of them and Marla said, "No Grady, you can't mean..."

Grady turned on his red lights and siren, and told Marla, "No matter what happens, stay down low!"

Marla slid down in her seat, as Grady reached for the mike of his radio and said, "Central from C-1."

"Go ahead C-1."

"You're not going to believe this, Mandy, but I'm in pursuit of the stolen blue sedan, license number 3485284. We're coming into Covenant from the North and we've just turned off of the expressway. See if you can get some units to set up a road block at the intersection of county roads 96 and 4B. We're now in excess of one-hundred miles per hour, Central."

"10-4 C-1! C-4, C-10 and County car #6 are responding and should be in position before you get there Chief."

"10-4 Central."

*   *   *

Warren, Grady's angel, and Long Blade, Marla's angel, had been working together to protect their human charges. They'd caused the bomb and the bomber's car to malfunction. Warren had played the part of the old man, while Long Blade had caused the bombers to see a wrecker and squad car where there were none!

Now they were helping Grady dodge deer and cars, which insisted on either running or pulling out in front of Grady's car. As the stolen car approached the roadblock, it began to slow down.

*   *   *

"Central, from C-1!"

"Go ahead, C-1."

"The vehicle is slowing down. All units be prepared to cut him off, if he tries to go around."

Grady heard several "10-4's" while his attention was on the sedan in front of him, which suddenly slammed on its brakes and made a 180 degree turn. Grady thought they'd try to ram his car, but instead, the suspect's car skidded sideways, the passenger jumped out firing his weapon at Grady's car as he did so!

Warren and Long Blade drew their swords and started deflecting the bullets causing them to whistle harmlessly past Grady's ears. They watched as Grady returned fire and the passenger went down. The driver then jumped out and fired a shotgun blast at Grady.

Grady caught the blast full in the chest and was thrown from his feet into the side of his squad car. Most of the double ought buckshot hit his bulletproof vest, but one embedded itself in Grady's right arm. As he slid to the ground, he lost feeling in his right arm and dropped his gun.

Just as the driver was taking aim to fire the other

barrel, C-4, a trained sniper, dropped the shooter with one clean shot through the head.

The Angels watched sadly as the men's souls were dragged kicking and screaming from their dead bodies by the very demons that had controlled them during their lifetimes.

The damned souls wailed and then disappeared beneath the asphalt road while the angels turned their attention back to Grady and Marla.

The entire firefight had lasted less than sixty seconds but it seemed like a lifetime. Grady was just noticing the blood, which began to run out from under his sleeve onto his 9mm. When Marla ran around the car and screamed!

The other officers were running up, calling for ambulances and the coroner.

Hankins, the sniper, walked over to Grady and said, as he handed two wallets to him, "I found these on the two dead shooters."

Grady, who'd been thinking of the shirt that had just been ruined took the ID's. He just stared at them for a full minute before he said, "Jesus help us! We've just killed two CIA agents!"

CHAPTER THIRTEEN
SARA'S PASSAGE

Sam Crawford lay on his cot holding Barb in his arms. She'd finally slipped into a merciful sleep about a half hour ago. Tears streamed silently down Sam's face as he remembered the events of this morning.

They'd been so happy after last night's healing meeting with Rev. Smith. Sam knew that he'd been healed. He felt it in his soul and so naturally, he and Barb had thought that their little Sara had also been healed. This morning however, when they'd happily taken her for the tests, which were supposed to confirm the healing, they were informed, that the brain tumor had doubled in size overnight and that Sara didn't have long to live. Unless a miracle occurred she would die within the week.

They were stunned! They had brought Sara here to get healed, not Sam!

Sam had stopped at the chapel on their way back to the tent and asked God to take his worthless life and to save Sara's. They had put Sara to bed when they returned to their tent home; she was very weak! Sam and Barb had been crying, as they tucked Sara in. Sara looked up, smiled weakly at them, and said, "Don't cry, Mommy. Daddy, everything's going to be all right. I've come here to die, because Jesus needs me! Andy told me that I'll have a really important job to do in heaven and that it'll be a lot of fun! He told me to be brave and I would soon be safe from all harm! I brought you here so

Jesus could help you, Daddy, and he has! I just knew he would!"

Barb asked, "Andy? Who's Andy, honey?"

Sara whispered as she fell asleep, "Oh, he's my guardian angel. He's real smart too! He knows everything!"

A chill ran down Barb's spine at her daughter's disturbing revelation. She kissed Sara's cheek, but she was already fast asleep!

"The innocence of a child!", thought Barb as she and her bewildered husband, dragged themselves to their own bed to mourn for their daughter. They felt so hopeless and anger was beginning to grow in their hearts. It was a bitterness that would soon fester into cold rage toward the heartless God, who would allow a sweet little girl like Sara to die! The Crawfords were about to learn that God cannot be manipulated into action, but rather, that all things are worked out according to His plans and in His time.

Just as Sam began to slip into a fitful sleep of his own, a movement caught his eye. He suddenly sat straight up, which caused Barb to wake with a start. The startled parents watched as Sara came skipping out of her room, holding the hand of a very handsome young man.

They stopped at the entrance of the tent, and Sara said, "I just wanted you to meet Andy before we leave. He really is nice, isn't he? I love you, Mommy and Daddy and please don't worry about me. I'll be just fine!"

With that, she and Andy skipped out of the tent.

Sam and Barb jumped up and ran out into the street, but they saw no one. Sam ran around the tent, while Barb ran to the corner looking both ways, frantically, as she went. They found nothing and met back at the entrance of their tent. Holding hands they went back in. They walked through the living room and into Sara's room with suspense and dread building with each step! They found her lifeless body lying peacefully where Sara had left it. Her eyes were open. Her frozen expression was one of awe at whatever vision she'd seen just at that last moment of life--when she was perfectly balanced between this world and the next.

Barb's screams of rage and pain could be heard all over the compound and they brought many concerned people to see what was wrong. There was great mourning and confusion; this was the second death this morning.

*   *   *

Dr. Kamerman sat at his desk and raised the second shot of whiskey to his lips, whispering as he did so, "It's impossible! It just can't be!"

He'd never really believed all this talk about Joshua's uncanny powers, until now.

He continued whispering to himself, "Mr. White apparently has some kind of power and I'm going to get that power for myself! Somehow!

"Get a hold of yourself, Doctor!", he demanded of himself.

His hands were still shaking as he downed the second shot and poured a third. As he drank it down, a plan formed in his deranged mind.

"That's it! I'll befriend Mr. White and get him to tell me his secrets. Then I'll help him see that all of this talk about angels, demons and miracles comes from the delusions that must be clouding his mind! I mean, to actually believe in invisible beings that can appear as people and help you in the here and now? No! Nor is there a God who's an actual being! There's just the cosmic force and everyone knows it! Well it's just too insane!"

The doctor suddenly yelled triumphantly, "God is mythological! Angels and demons are mythological! I'll show you the error of your ways, Mr. White! I'll find out just how you're tapping into the cosmic force and using its power. Then I'll take that power and use it myself!"

The doctor hit the intercom button, triumphantly, and yelled, "Bring Mr. White to my office, right away!"

*   *   *

Jarrett White had just pulled out of the State Park when he heard the sirens. He watched as a car sped by followed closely by a police car in hot pursuit. He watched from the entrance of the park and pulled out behind the pursuit following to see what would happen. From the top of a hill, he watched as a firefight raged brutally below him.

As a sniper, Officer Hankins, took out the second shooter, an idea formed in Jarrett's mind. He saw that these police officers were professionals; a head-on attack wouldn't be necessary, but rather, a subtler plan could be used.

Jarrett White, as he was getting used to calling himself, again, turned his new white motorcycle around and headed back to his men. The plan solidified in his mind and he smiled.

Jarrett whispered, "I'll return as I left, surrounded in mystery."

Jarrett White knew it was time for him to end his mission, when he saw the two fellow CIA Agents shot. He knew they were dirty and tied up in Dr. Kamerman's plans, even if he didn't know just how. It was time for "Eagle" to come home to roost. It was time for him to get in contact with Richard Aires, Director of the CIA.

*   *   *

Lt. Crygen, Tumult's right hand man, stood before Captain Rumpus, Dr. Kamerman's own personal demon and ruler over all of Washington D.C. They were meeting in Rumpus' battle and strategy chamber.

Capt. Rumpus looked down from his throne, and said, *"Well, Lt. Crygen, to what do I owe this unexpected and uninvited pleasure?"*

His voice fairly dripped with menace and suppressed anger. A weaker messenger would've cringed under Rumpus's glare, but this was Lt. Crygen, a demon with many battles behind him. He lived without fear of any demon and respected only Tumult and Satan, himself.

Crygen bowed slightly, just a little too slightly, and replied, "I bring you greetings from Capt. Tumult, who..."

Capt. Rumpus interrupted Lt. Crygen, *"And why isn't Tumult here himself paying me homage?"*

Lt. Crygen offered, "Unlike you, sir, Tumult doesn't have time to sit around on his throne. He has too much work to do!" Capt. Rumpus stood up and shouted, "Kill this impertinent swine!"

Two guards attacked Crygen instantly and it was quite unfortunate for them. Before they could even get to him, Crygen had already pulled his own sword and with movements quicker than Rumpus could follow, Crygen slew the two guards and suddenly had the razor sharp blade of his sword resting against the throat of Rumpus, himself.

Lt. Crygen whispered contempt to the terrified Rumpus, "Now, sir, if you'll be kind enough to call off your ghouls, I'll let you live...*this time*!"

The calm with which he spoke sent tremors of fear creeping down Rumpus' spine, burrowing deep into his already terrified heart. He quickly signaled to his men to back off. Lt. Crygen let his blade move across Rumpus's throat leaving a beaded, crimson line in its place.

Crygen affirmed, as he re-sheathed his sword, "That should leave just enough of a scar, that you'll be reminded from time to time how lucky you were this day.

"Now to the business at hand! Tumult has sent me here to inform you, officially, that he's taking full command over all operations in this world. Handed down via Satan's personal directions, which I believe you'll find, are in perfect order.

"He's mounting an offensive that'll send fear into the hearts of the angels, who think that they have Covenant secure. They even think that they're gaining ground in the United States of America, but they are mistaken!"

Capt. Rumpus found his courage, and said, "Wait just a minute! I run the American Operation! It was my men who captured this Joshua White; a man that your people couldn't seem to kill! While you allowed him to save the President and inflict other harm on our kingdom, we've captured both the President and Joshua White, and are in the process of turning them to our side!"

Crygen laughed, "Yes, Yes! We know all about your feeble attempts in this area and you may continue them until ordered to do other more important things when Tumult arrives here in a couple of hours.

"I'm just here to tell you to be ready at a moment's notice to relinquish your command to Tumult and to follow his orders to the letter!"

Rumpus stood, *"And what if I don't want that incompetent failure to get my men killed needlessly?"*

Crygen laughed, "Then you'd be challenging the demon who has personally received "The Jewel of Authority" from our Lord Satan himself! If that's the case, would you like to use swords or daggers when you meet him? Tumult will want to know."

Capt. Rumpus's legs buckled and he sat down, the color draining from his face, as beads of sweat formed on his brow. He knew that Tumult had been given the task of defeating the Christians of Covenant, again, but he didn't know that he'd been given, "The Jewel of Authority"!

He'd already insulted the emissary of Satan's most powerful demon, which, in itself, might yet get him killed, but to directly challenge Tumult would be suicide!

Rumpus stood again. His demeanor totally changed.

"Lt. Crygen, let's start over shall we? These are trying times and we need to work together not against each other. Come, let me show you around."

Rumpus walked down from his throne and put a

brotherly arm around Crygen, who good-naturedly allowed himself to be led deeper into Rumpus' territory.

Rumpus bragged, "Let me show you, Lt. Crygen, just what we've accomplished over the last few years. The Committee has been extremely busy helping our Lord Satan to get control of, not only The United States, but many other countries in the world. We're getting ready, as you know, for the time of the Antichrist which if plans go well, could be sooner than we anticipated!"

No sooner had the words left Rumpus' mouth than a cool gentle breeze whispered through their midst. Instantly they felt the great powers of evil stirring restlessly as God put plans of His own into action.

*   *   *

Rev. Smith knocked and then entered the Crawford tent. As he entered, Barb looked at him with hollow eyes, which widened while at the same time she jumped up and started pounding on his shoulders with both hands.

She screamed, "You promised that our little girl would be cured! You said that all we needed was faith and she'd be spared! Now she's dead! *What did we do wrong? Why does God hate us so much?"*

She wept as Sam grabbed her and held her to his chest.

Tears were streaming unashamedly from his own eyes as he said to Rev. Smith, "I'm sorry, Pastor, but we're beside ourselves with grief! We don't understand! We know that hundreds were saved at the meeting last night and many were healed, including myself. Why didn't God take my miserable life instead of my sweet Sara's? I asked him; no, I begged him to take me and let her live, but he has turned a deaf ear to my cry as usual!"

Rev. Smith prayed for guidance but didn't receive much in the way of inspiration.

He said, "First of all Barb, Sam; God isn't punishing you -- he loves you very much and that I can tell you from first hand experience! He loves you so much that he allowed Sara to say good-bye before she left. He also allowed you to meet her guardian angel, Andy, which should encourage you as to her true condition."

Sam began to protest, but Rev. Smith held up his hand and said, "Look, I don't have all of the answers, but I do have some experiences that I can share with you. I've known Joshua White for years. I've seen him die and I've seen God raise him from the dead. He described the death experience not as a gloomy, sad experience; but on the contrary, he said that it's a beautiful and warm experience! From what I've heard of your experience with Sara, you know this to be true. Sara was smiling even in death. Her soul was happy, bouncing and in the presence of her guardian angel! This is knowledge that should comfort you both very much! Sara is at home with Jesus, doing her important job for our Lord!

"Joshua once told me that when someone dies, he or she is wrapped in a beautiful pure light filled with warmth and love and taken directly to the Lord Jesus, Himself. I really can't describe the feelings that he had except by using the word ecstatic. Recall the moments in your own lives when you had such feelings that you thought, "It doesn't get any better than this!" Now take that feeling and enhance it a million fold and you still won't be close to the feelings that Joshua said he felt while in heaven with the Lord. Jesus did tell Joshua, during his visit, that death is not a punishment or even a bad thing. No real harm is done. In fact, the person is freed from the prison of the body. Jesus told him that every person is given so much time on earth and that those years are determined and set by the Father before we're even born. That's why, when people die and show up in heaven before their time, they're usually told that they're not finished yet; go back and finish up!

"In the case of your daughter, Sara, her time was up regardless of what we say or do. We must remember, therefore, that we're eternal creations of God and once he creates our soul and puts it into our body, at the time of our conception, we never really die from that point on. We're to grow in His Love and Salvation. Then when it's our time to begin our duties in heaven, we're simply changed.

"What we call death is really no more than our real birth into eternal, unlimited and overwhelming joy. Look! I know that without personally experiencing this, it's hard for us to imagine all of these things, but endeavor to believe what I say to you to be true. Let's pray together that God will show you what to do with this painful experience, for..."

Sam spoke up bitterly, "I already know what He can do with it! *He can. . .*"

"Now Sam I know you are hurting but you mustn't take it out on God. He can take it of course but you'll feel sorry later for calling him names. Any one of us would be angry, even with God and He understands that, but you must understand that God loves you and He is going through this with you."

Rev. Smith grabbed Sam by the shoulders and held him firmly in place, looked into his eyes and said in a whisper, "We all love you Sam and we loved Sara but she has gone on to her reward and she came here so that you could go on to yours one day. She told me that herself, Sam. She was only concerned with your soul, Sam. Now please calm down Sam and let's pray together for strength, peace and that calmness that only God's Spirit can bring to us."

They prayed together and Sam calmed down quite a bit before Rev. Smith said, "Now, let's go to my office and I'll help you with the funeral arrangements."

They left others to prepare Sara's body for the burial while Sam bravely began to answer the Pastor's questions, as they walked toward his office.

*   *   *

As Andy left the tent with Sara's sweet soul, he transformed into his full angelic glory and wrapping Sara in his wings he began the journey through the many veils that separate this world from the next.

Sara was filled with such an overpowering love and joy that she had nothing with which to compare it, therefore, she just relished it. Knowledge began to fill her soul and she was far beyond her five years of experience by the time they arrived in Heaven.

When Andy unfurled his wings to expose Sara to her Lord Jesus, it was not a little five-year-old girl that he uncovered. In her place was the form of a beautiful young woman of about thirty years of age.

Of course, this surprised neither Jesus nor Andy.

Sara, however, seemed very confused, even uneasy. Jesus smiled and held his arms out and Sara fairly threw herself into them. As soon as he embraced her, all the missing pieces fell into place and Sara knew that everyone in heaven appears to be about thirty years old-- it really makes little difference since none of them really have a body anyway, but rather they are made of light. This revelation made little difference to Sara because everything seemed real enough and she knew what it was that the Lord had in mind for her to do and she couldn't wait to get started!

Jesus spoke, "Ah, my blessed Sara, welcome to your eternal home. Before you begin your joyful task for your God, my Father wants to greet you Himself. You'll finally get to see Him as He really is!"

Jesus turned to Andy and said, "You've done a fine job, Andy, now go to Michael and receive your new orders."

Andy moved his right hand to his left shoulder in the salute of respect and watched as Jesus put his arm around Sara leading her through the gate of 'New Jerusalem'. As they both began to fade into the pure light of God the Father, Andy heard Sara's distant sigh of awe and wonder. Andy could feel Sara's happiness as she disappeared into the pure love that is God. With a happy heart, Andy flew with angelic speed and appeared almost instantly before Michael, the Archangel.

Michael looked up and said, "Ah, Andy, welcome home! You've done a fine job and I'd like to offer you another assignment if you're willing to take one on so soon."

Andy nodded his acceptance.

"Now I warn you, this will not be an easy assignment, nor a satisfying one, but it is important to our overall plans.

"I know you can handle this, if you care to!"

Andy said, "You know I live to serve our Lord Jesus! I'll do whatever I can to help. Please tell me what it is that I'm to do."

Michael smiled, "I knew you'd be right for this job! Now listen, here's what I need. There's a man named Jarrett White down on earth, and I want you to..."

CHAPTER FOURTEEN

THE ENEMY'S LAIR

"Ye have heard that it hath been said, Thou shalt love thy neighbor, and hate thine enemy. But I say unto you, Love your enemies, bless them that curse you, do good to them that hate you, and pray for them which despitefully use you, and persecute you;..."

"Shut up!", the guard said, as he pushed Joshua into Dr. Kamerman's office.

Joshua had been praying Matthew 5:43-44 over and over all the way from his cell trying to remind himself to love his enemies but the guard had had enough!

The first thing Joshua noticed after stumbling into the office, was the fact that it was neat...too neat. It looked as though everything had its place and to prove the point Dr. Kamerman was turning a paperweight to that particular angle which, apparently, made him feel more comfortable. Joshua also noticed the doctor had labeled his desk mate so that the bin which held the paper clips was marked "paper clips" and the staples were marked "staples", etc., as if you couldn't see what they held. The entire room was like that! In fact, it reminded Joshua of a blueprint on which one labels each piece of furniture and where it might go or a giant jigsaw puzzle where each item in the room fits into another item. It spoke volumes to Joshua about the man who he now faced.

Dr. Kamerman got up, walked around the desk and indicated a chair, which Joshua noticed sat lower to the floor than the one Dr. Kamerman had chosen for himself. Joshua chuckled at all the little signs indicating Dr. Kamerman's need to control his environment.

Dr. Kamerman said, "Come in, Mr. White, and relax for awhile."

"Said the spider to the fly," Joshua thought, as he took the offered seat and found it to be quite comfortable though a bit low to the floor.

He said, "Where's the couch, Doc?"

The doctor smiled, "That's old fashion, Mr. White. No, today we feel that sitting face to face is a better way to read the whole person so we can discover how to help them."

Joshua smiled back, "I agree, Doctor, that this is better; but if you wanted to talk to me, you could've called or stopped by. It wasn't necessary to kidnap me, torture me and then, what, psychoanalyze me?"

The doctor said, uncomfortably, "Those are harsh words about the person who's trying to bring you back to your senses, Mr. White."

Joshua smiled, "No, Dr. Kamerman, they're not harsh words just truthful. I've been thinking if you have the power to send a cleansing unit to pick me up, then you must have powerful ties with the CIA."

Dr. Kamerman nodded his head, "Very good, Mr. White! I was told you're very intelligent and that you catch on quickly. It's a shame, however, that you've chosen to follow this outdated mythological religion you call Christianity. It's already cost you a wonderful career with our government!" The doctor leaned forward and added just a touch of malice to his voice, as he whispered, "And may, if you don't reject it, cost you your life!"

Joshua stood up, causing the Doctor to sit back quickly. Ignoring the Doctor's statement, as well as the Doctor himself, Joshua walked over to a book shelf and slowly, meticulously picked up each book or knickknack and purposely put it down in the wrong place.

He said, "Why do you assume, Doctor, that Jesus is a myth?"

Without consciously thinking about it Dr. Kamerman got up and followed behind Joshua putting everything back into it's exact and proper place. The Doctor's discomfort was growing, both from the strain caused by his neatness phobia and this talk about Jesus.

Dr. Kamerman said, "Mr. White! How can you possibly follow a man like Jesus? True, he lived an obscure life two thousand years ago, but utterly failed! His followers deserted him at the first sign of trouble! The people hated him enough to have him arrested and put to death! You do know that he died, don't you, Mr. White?"

Smiling at his own sarcasm Dr. Kamerman went on, "This is where the myth part comes in. His followers decided to hide his body and then to act as if he'd risen from the dead. They spread rumors that they'd seen and talked to him after his supposed resurrection and there were many foolish people who believed the myth until it became truth to their deceived minds. That deception was then passed down through the generations and has infected even a man of your obvious training and intelligence! How can you believe the insane ranting of this long dead false prophet, Mr. White?"

Joshua started to answer, but Dr. Kamerman cut him off. "Look, Mr. White, I know you have great power and that it comes, not from this Jesus, but from the Cosmic Force which permeates the universe. What I want to know is how you tap into this power whenever you like so as to do all of the miraculous things I've heard you've done? Come; tell me Mr. White, so we can be partners! There's plenty of power in the universe for both of us!"

Joshua looked up from the crystal ball he was holding in his hands and said, "I suppose you use this and your Ouija board over there to get predictions about the future. I suppose you even consult these things for current business affairs as well."

He could see by the doctor's expression that he "of course" did just that!

"Is it your belief that these items can tap into this universal force of which you speak so highly?"

A nervous Dr. Kamerman took the crystal ball, replaced it in its stand saying, "Yes, these things help in smaller matters, but I want the power you have, Mr. White! Teach me how to tap into your quality of power and I'll set you free!"

He carefully took Joshua by the arm, led him back to his chair, then resumed his own seat saying, as he did so, "Come Mr. White what's your secret? What incantations do you chant? What formulas do you follow to accomplish these great things? I, like you, just want to make the world a better place to live!"

As the doctor looked at him expectantly, Joshua crossed his right leg over his left and said, "Dr. Kamerman, there is no secret and I'll gladly share this power with you!"

Dr. Kamerman sat forward in his chair, chewing his lower lip in anticipation, as Joshua continued, "All of my power comes from the Lord, Jesus Christ, and his Holy Spirit! I don't control or channel the power, as you people believe you do! Instead, I simply love the person, ask for God's compassion to be shown and then I accept God's answer, even if He says, "No!". God created the entire universe, everything in it and wields His power at His Will, not ours! We, Christians, don't chant incantations or use formulas or curses to tap into God's power! We simply pray to know God's Will and then follow His Will even unto death!

"Dr. Kamerman, you people don't tap into the Universal Force as you call it, but rather you open yourselves up to demonic possession and the power of Satan! They let you think you're controlling them; yet, they slowly and very patiently take over your souls! They'll eventually destroy you and your soul! If you continue on this path, doctor, you'll end up in the tar pits of Hell! I've seen them and they aren't a pleasant sight. I don't want to see you end up there! So please, accept the truth! Accept Jesus into your life! I can then teach you all about the power of God's Spirit in our lives! What do you say?" It was Josh's turn to sit on the edge of his seat in anticipation.

Dr. Kamerman just stared at Joshua, disappointment leaking into his expression. He was at a total loss of words and had no simple way to pierce Joshua's faith.

*   *   *

Capt. Rumpus was enjoying Dr. Kamerman's discomfort with his neatness phobia, but Joshua was beginning to make him uncomfortable with all of this talk about Jesus. Rumpus, therefore, tightened his grip on Dr. Kamerman's brain and spinal column, causing his long gnarled yellowish-gray claws to disappear beneath the doctor's flesh.

The Captain leaned forward and whispered, with an evil smile, "Show him the President!"

Rumpus then began to pump feelings of superiority into the doctor's soul...

*   *   *

Dr. Kamerman shook off his disappointment. He smiled, stood up, walked over to the bookshelves behind his desk and pushing a hidden button, caused the bookshelves to separate in the middle. Half of the shelf slid in one direction while the other half slid in the opposite direction. When the shelves had fully parted, they exposed a large bank of T.V. screens. It had one large screen in the middle, surrounded by smaller screens, three on each side as well as across the top and bottom, twelve in all.

At first Joshua couldn't tell what he was seeing on the screens. It finally registered that he was watching several cells, like the one he'd just come from. The scene changed and all of the screens showed the same picture. Realization came slowly to Joshua, but what he saw turned his stomach into a pit of acid, which rose slowly into his burning throat.

He saw a half dressed woman hanging from the ceiling. He could see that her muscles were all one big bundle of painful knots. Just as Joshua was about to ask the doctor how he could treat another human being like this, the victim's identity finally registered upon his consciousness. Joshua found himself looking into the inverted face of President Roberta Place.

Joshua's first impulse as he turned toward Dr. Kamerman was to beat this man to a pulp...

*   *   *

Captain Rumpus was overjoyed at Joshua's reaction! He could smell Joshua's hatred and licked his lips in anticipation, hoping that Joshua would murder the doctor, thus damning both the doctor and himself to Hell. A split second later, however, Joshua's hatred was replaced with shame and then compassion.

Captain Rumpus watched in horror as Joshua knelt down on the office floor and began to pray for Dr. Kamerman, "Lord Jesus forgive my anger and hatred. Free Dr. Kamerman from the demons that possess him. Help me to pray for my enemies as you instructed me in Matthew 5:43-44. In the name of Jesus Christ I demand that the demons that possess Dr. Kamerman leave him, immediately! Help the doctor to fight this enemy from within, as we all must, and..."

As Joshua prayed, lightening struck at Rumpus from the ceiling as Aaron streaked in with his naked blade aimed at the heart of the dark lord. Rumpus was forced to rip himself free of Dr. Kamerman and draw his own sword, but he was too late to totally block Aaron's advance. Aaron's sword pierced Rumpus' side spilling the first blood.

The captain recovered quickly, however, and yelled

at the doctor to stop White and then fought back fiercely.

As they fought, Aaron spoke through his strained effort, "You'll lose this attack on the Christians, just as Tumult lost the Battle of Covenant! The more you attack them, the more they will pray for your demise. You've already lost thousands of your troops to just a handful of Christians! What do you suppose might happen, if say, a few thousand or even a few million Christians prayed for their enemies?!"

The sparks flew as their blades ripped at each other in an attempt to send one or the other back to his Master. After several minutes of fighting, the two supernatural beings stood panting and glaring at each other.

*　　*　　*

Dr. Kamerman was frightened when he saw the hatred in Joshua's eyes, he knew the look of murder when he saw it! He froze! He caught his hand reaching for the warning buzzer that would bring the guards. Instead of attacking, however, Mr. White knelt on the floor and started praying for him.

The doctor's heart was pounding and he suddenly got a terrible headache. At first Dr. Kamerman was embarrassed, then uncomfortable and finally frightened. He didn't know why Joshua's words frightened him, but he knew he must stop him! The doctor finally found the courage and pushed the alarm button. The doors burst open and two guards stormed in. Without hesitation they swung their clubs hitting Joshua in the head. Then, they unceremoniously dragged his bleeding unconscious body from the doctor's office.

*   *   *

After resting for a moment, Aaron took the initiative and attacked Rumpus. Both warriors were bleeding profusely from both the serious and not so serious wounds they'd inflicted on one another. They were both getting weaker. Ignoring the pain, they clashed in a mighty clanging of steel, their thunderous power echoed throughout the chamber. The flashing of unnatural lightening caused their eerie shadows to dance on the walls and across the ceiling.

Aaron brought his blade down hard causing Rumpus to trip, loose his footing and fall attempting to block the blow. Landing on his back he felt Aaron's blade dig deeply into the side of his neck and that's when Rumpus decided that he'd had enough, disappearing in disgraceful retreat.

Aaron watched, sadly, as they dragged Joshua from the room. Aaron then turned and touched Dr. Kamerman's eyes saying, "Watch this doctor!"

*   *   *

Dr. Kamerman felt very strange and a bit dizzy as he sat down facing the monitors.

"Just adrenaline, I guess", he whispered.

He thought he'd watch the President's agony for a moment, but what he saw made him turn even paler than he had already become. Then he gasped!

The doctor watched as two translucent angelic beings lowered the President to the floor, clothed her in a beautiful white gown and from thin air, handed her a loaf of hot bread and a cup of some kind of steaming liquid.

Dr. Kamerman rubbed his eyes and when he looked again the two beings of light were gone with the President sitting on her bunk, much as Joshua had earlier, eating the food that seemed to be healing all of her wounds. She looked refreshed and beautiful in a way that the doctor would never understand.

It was a trembling Dr. Kamerman who sat back in his chair and wept.

He said, "I'm losing it! I'm finally cracking up!"

The doctor babbled, drooled and wept well into the afternoon...

CHAPTER FIFTEEN
MENDING BROKEN LIVES

There was a slight drizzle making the exhausted Crawfords chilly causing them to pull the collars up on their coats as they got out of the car. Sara had died just two days ago, seeming like a lifetime to the weary couple. The funeral director did his best to keep the umbrella over their heads as Sam helped Barb from the car and they walked together behind Sara's casket. Sam shivered as some rain poured off of the umbrella and down his neck. They hurried to get under the tent and Sam thought about all they'd been through wishing it was about over. They had a wonderful visitation for Sara last night with many people coming by to see them. They'd all been very kind and it had helped to lift both Sam and Barb's spirits.

A stranger had come up to Sam last night and offered him a job working on the new high-rise buildings, currently under construction in Jesus Park. He'd looked at Barb, she'd nodded her approval and he accepted. He'd start in a couple of days, after they had time to mourn for Sara. Sam couldn't believe people were helping him, even after he'd told them everything he was supposed to do. Not only did they give him a job, but Rev. Smith had told them last night that all of Sam's gambling debts had been paid and now he was off the hook. A lawyer had asked if Sam would sign a statement that Starvas Creen had intimidated him to murder Rev. Smith and, of course, he did. His life had changed overnight and even Barb, had been offered a job helping with the day care center fulfilling her wish to be around children.

Now, however, they faced the crushing reality and finality of burying little Sara. The funeral director sat them down in the front row on folding chairs. The chairs were covered with green velvet, which made them warmer. After seating them, the funeral director laid a blanket on their laps, which brought welcome relief to their damp chilled bones.

As people poured into the tent all around them, the Crawfords looked at their daughter's little pink coffin. It was on a stand centered over the hole into which they'd soon lower Sara's body. There it would remain until such time as the Lord returned to claim His Church. The dirt pile was covered with fake, green grass and all the flowers from the visitation. The casket flowers were roses splashed with baby's breath and plenty of greenery. Everything looked so beautiful and yet so cold! As they sat there looking at the casket, each parent, independent of the other, wanted to rip the casket open and get one last hug, knowing that it was hopeless.

Barb began to feel overwhelmed by her grief once again. In an attempt to get her mind off her own sorrow, she watched as a little black girl was carried from the car to another tent set up just across from where she was sitting. Barb never gave a thought to the girl's color, but rather her heart was breaking at seeing the girl's expression of pain and fear.

Last night they'd found out that a Mr. Patterson had died earlier on the same day as Sara. His wife had died in a car wreck last year; a victim of a drunk driver. Just six months ago Mr. Patterson had a heart attack.

He'd come here for a cure so he could take care of his little Geraldine. What made it really sad was the fact that neither he nor his deceased wife had any living relatives. Geraldine would be totally alone!

No one really understood why some people weren't healed when they asked. There were already twelve graves here in Jesus Park, counting Mr. Patterson and Sara, to prove that they weren't all healed.

Barb was proud of the brave way that Geraldine was handling herself and thought if Sara had been in Geraldine's position, she'd also have been brave. Barb snuggled closer to Sam as the Pastor continued the service with, "...ashes to ashes, dust to dust..."

Barb was now crying as much for Geraldine as she was for her own loss and then, just like that, it was over!

Barb suddenly cried out, "No! Please let me say good-bye!"

Everyone looked sympathetically at Barb and made room for her to approach the casket.

She rested her hands on Sara's casket, pulled off some flower petals and sprinkled them on the casket. She wept! Then she fought as Sam began to pull her away from the casket. She didn't want to leave! Barb was suddenly filled with wide-eyed desperate panic. She wanted this moment to be frozen, so she wouldn't have to let go. Then they were again walking under the umbrella with the rain driving hard against it. The funeral director led them toward the waiting car. Barb gave in to hopelessness as she forever left her little girl in God's hands.

As they walked, Barb heard someone cry out, "No honey, don't bother those poor people!"

Sam stopped. They both looked toward the other tent and saw the little girl running toward them. She was fast and very determined for a girl of four years. She reached the Crawfords just before the pursuing adults. The adults were close, only because Geraldine had fallen twice in the wet grass on the way over, but the adults were much more winded than Geraldine appeared to be.

One of the adults picked the girl up, trying to balance her on one arm and her umbrella on the other, as she said, "We're very sorry for the intrusion, but she insisted on telling you something! We're sorry for your loss, please excuse us; we'll leave you alone now!"

As they began to walk away, the struggling Geraldine yelled, "No! I must tell them what Sara told me last night! I promised!"

When Barb heard Sara's name, she stopped, turned in Sam's arms and yelled, "Wait! I want to hear what Geraldine has to say!"

The adult that was carrying Geraldine shrugged her shoulders and set the girl down allowing her to run into Barb's outstretched arms. The director tried to protect them both from the now torrential rains, but he was losing the battle. As Barb knelt in the wet grass she ignored the chill that ran through her. Geraldine, however, was shaking uncontrollably not only from the cold rain, but from the emotional strain that her father's death and Sara's visitation had caused her.

Barb removed her own jacket, wrapped Geraldine in its warmth and whispered softly to her, "What is it, honey? What do you need to tell me?"

Through sobs of exhaustive sorrow Geraldine whispered, "Last night a beautiful lady was by my bed.

She told me her name was Sara and that she'd been a little girl just yesterday, but she'd grown up already. She said everyone is grown up in Heaven. She told me she was worried about her own mommy and daddy, and asked if I'd help her. Well, she was very nice and very, very pretty; so, of course, I wanted to help!

"First though, she told me that my own mommy and daddy are together again and they're very happy in heaven. That made me feel really good!

"Then she told me I should come to you at the funeral and tell you not to worry about her, she's enjoying very important work and a wonderful new life with Jesus!

"She also asked me if I'd offer myself, you know, as a substitute daughter."

Geraldine grabbed Barb's lapels, looked her right in the eyes and pleaded, "I told her I'm black and white folk wouldn't want no black girl for a daughter!

"But Sara only laughed and told me that in Heaven all color is respected equally so it doesn't matter what color we are down here. My Daddy always told me that I shouldn't hate anyone for any reason, especially for the color of his or her skin. He'd always told me that we have the same color tongue, heart and blood. Daddy told me we only have different colored skin to add to the beauty and wonder of God's creation.

"Anyway, Sara told me she was afraid that her mommy would miss reading those bedtime stories and she would be sad. She said her daddy might get angry and bitter if he didn't have someone to love!"

Geraldine asked for a Kleenex and was offered several; one from each of the many people who were listening intently to her story. She was sobbing deeper now, as she wiped her eyes on the Kleenex that Barb offered her and then blew her nose.

She then looked into Barb's eyes, again, and said, "I think you'd make a mighty nice mommy!"

Barb's own eyes filled with tears and her heart swelled with compassion as she hugged her looking up at Sam with a mixture of hope and fear. Sam was very prejudiced against black people and Barb feared he would refuse to consider adopting Geraldine. Sam, however, was shaking and tears were running down his cheeks.

He fell to his knees and wept, as he pulled Geraldine and Barb to him and said, "Maybe we should help heal each other?"

Geraldine hugged his neck and without a word Sam picked her up and helping Barb to her feet said, "Shall we get our daughter out of this rain, honey?"

Barb jumped up and down and laughed, "Yes! Oh, Yes! Thank you God! Thank you Sam!"

Together they walked to the car, with the funeral director still, stubbornly, trying to keep the rain off of their heads even though they were all already soaked to the skin.

Tears mixed with rain as the people around them began to applaud and cheer. They cheered for the love and compassion they'd just witnessed. They cheered for God's love and for the rainbow that had just appeared in the Eastern sky as the rain began to let up. Finally, they cheered for the loving God who'd saved them all!

*   *   *

Standing, not far away, but unseen by human eyes, was Mr. and Mrs. Patterson and Sara. Tears of joy streamed down their smiling faces as they streaked into the sky on their way back to Heaven. They could now give their entire attention to their work knowing that their families would be loved and cared for until they were all together again in Heaven.

*   *   *

Rev. Smith had watched this wonderful scene and was now praising God for His wisdom. Only God could take these occasions of grief and pain and turn them into hopeful joy. He then motioned to Jeb Johnson. Jeb was a lawyer, who'd just been cured of leukemia, started walking toward Rev. Smith.

As he approached, Rev. Smith asked, "Say Jeb, could you...?"

"Don't even need to ask Pastor. I'll be happy to draw up the necessary papers to make the adoption legal and binding. They make a nice looking family, don't they?"

"That they do, Jeb. That they do!"

The men shook hands and Rev. Smith walked over to his car. He got in and headed for the Covenant Police Department, to check on Grady.

CHAPTER SIXTEEN

YOU KNOW THE DRILL

Grady was nervous! It had been a full day since the shooting of the two CIA agents. He hadn't heard a word from their superiors. When he had called to inform them of the incident, they had basically just listened. They said they'd be in touch and that was it! No shock, no sadness, not even any anger, just a "We'll be in touch" and they hung up! He'd figured they surely would have been in touch by now.

Grady had ordered an autopsy done on both men and had the full report in the seat next to him. Cause of death "multiple gun shot wounds." It contained nothing else of interest.

Grady turned to Marla, and said, "That prayer service was great Marla, but I'm too nervous to enjoy the blessings we just experienced! It's making me nervous that I haven't heard anything yet."

"Yeah, they don't seem to be very interested in their own men, do they?"

"That's what makes me nervous! They either don't care or they're really taking time to plan their course of action. It could get rough for me and the department, either way!"

"Just remember, Grady, these agents are the ones who stole a car, drove like crazy men and then started shooting at you without cause!"

"I know you're right Marla, but the CIA seems to have the power to do just about anything they want!

They may not be forced to make sense or explain their actions and I'm just not sure what they can do to us. But not hearing from them and having to guess what might happen is bothering me more than anything!" They were silent as Grady pulled up to Marla's apartment building.

Marla questioned, "Do you want to come up and talk for awhile, honey?"

"If you don't mind, I think I'll just go home and take a shower then go to bed. I'm beat!"

Leaning over and kissing Grady tenderly, Marla said, "Does that help, sweety?"

Grady smiled put his left arm around her, his right arm was in a sling from his wound, as they kissed passionately. He then whispered, "Yes honey, that helped very much! Do you want me to walk you up?"

"No, I'll be fine. You just go home and get some rest."

He gave her one last hug then Marla got out of the car and walked into her building. Grady watched her enter the building then turned his car toward home.

On the way, Grady's thoughts turned toward Sara Crawford and Mr. Patterson. He'd hated missing their funerals, but he'd been in the emergency room getting patched up from his gunshot wound at the time. Rev. Smith had told Grady and Marla about the services and he'd shared the story of how the Crawfords were going to adopt Geraldine. Grady and Marla had an opportunity to meet them after the service and they did appear very happy!

Just then Grady's car phone rang.

"Hello."

"Grady, this is Mandy at the station. There are

three men here claiming to be CIA agents! They're certainly dressed for the part. All three are wearing black suits. I told them to wait in the lobby, but they're in your office going through your desk and filing cabinets! I'm sorry I just don't know what to do!"

"Which of our officers are there right now, Mandy?"

As she went to check anger began to replace Grady's nervousness. He liked his privacy and he didn't care who they were, they had no business in his office!

Mandy came back on just a little out of breath, "Hankins is here, but Grady, those men have physically dragged him into your office and closed the door! Phillips and Romero are both on patrol."

"All right, Mandy, have them report to me at post, I'm on my way!"

He made a squealing U-turn and headed for the station.

When he arrived at the station, he stopped by the radio room and checked in with Mandy.

Grady smiled, and got down to business, "Are they still in my office?"

"I think so. It was scary, Grady. They took Jimmy's gun and pushed him into your office! They were very rough, mean and obnoxiously rude!"

"OK, I'll take care of it! Have Phillips and Romero report to me in my office when they arrive."

Grady was dressed in slacks, white shirt and tie. His shoulder holster was hidden by the right side of his jacket, as was the 9mm Beretta that it held. He'd borrowed a left-handed holster and was thankful that he'd insisted on learning how to shoot equally well with both hands. The right side of his jacket was thrown over and pinned to his sling with the borrowed holster cradled snugly beneath his sling. As Grady walked up to his office, he could see through the wall of glass that made up the front of his office. He saw one man looking through his files, while another was holding a gun on Hankins and the third was right in his face, yelling! Grady didn't stop at his door, but turned the handle and hit the door with his shoulder expecting to enter. It was locked! The impact wasn't great, but it was enough to hurt his right arm causing it to throb again.

Grady lost his temper and yelled, "Open this door, you're in my office!"

The man whose face was nose to nose with Hankins turned and yelled back, "Go away! We'll get to you later!"

Grady pulled his gun out with his left hand, sending a bolt of pain through his right arm, and fired twice at the lock. He then kicked the door open and leveled the gun on the man who'd been pointing his gun at Hankins, but who'd now turned to aim at Grady as he entered.

At that moment, Phillips and Romero entered, on the run, each brandishing a riot scattergun. Riot scatterguns lay down a broad pattern and one couldn't miss at this range. By now the other two CIA agents had pulled their guns and, were sweeping them back and forth, from one officer to another not quite sure what to do.

Grady ordered, "Officer Hankins come over here."

The CIA agent who'd been grilling him, pushed him back into his seat with his free hand and said, "We aren't finished with this man yet Mr..."

"It's Chief O'Leary, and yes, you are finished here!

You can't come into my office, go through my records, push my people around and then expect any kind of cooperation! I want..."

"Chief, I'm not interested in what you want! You shot two of my men and I'll do whatever I want to find the truth as to why you did that! You people of Covenant have been under investigation for a long time and it's a well-known fact that you don't like the government. We..."

Grady's face was getting as red as his hair, a very dangerous sign and his men knew it. The CIA men weren't smart enough to notice.

Grady yelled, "You can start your investigation with your own men! Tell me why they were following me? Why my car had a bomb in it, that luckily malfunctioned or I'd be dead? Tell me why they stole a car from the airport and why they ran from me when I tried to apprehend them? Then you can, finally, tell me why they started shooting at my men and me when we did stop them?"

Grady was shaking with anger. His nerves were shot! The man by the filing cabinet said, "At ease Bob."

These words were directed to the man who had been grilling Hankins. The man hesitated, but then he slowly put his gun away. Then both of the other CIA men did the same.

Grady stood there for a moment longer, trying to calm his nerves. He finally put his own gun away, then told all three of his men to wait for him outside.

As they left, Grady said, "Hankins, would you bring a pot of coffee in here and then I want all three of you to hang around, especially you," he pointed to Hankins.

They left and Grady turned his attention back to his "guests". He walked around his desk, sat down behind it and motioned them to sit in the chairs on the other side.

Grady was still angry and said a little coldly, "Now, maybe you'll explain to me what's going on?"

The man who'd defused the situation spoke first. Grady figured him to be in his late fifties. He had gray-streaked hair and wore wire-rim glasses. The other men were younger, but there was nothing distinctly different about any of them. Grady figured it must be the attire.

The man said, "Chief O'Leary, I'm Richard Aires, Director of the CIA and a good friend of President Place. This is my assistant, Bob Swaggert". He indicated the man who'd grilled Hankins, "And this, is Special Agent George Jones, in charge of covert operations." He indicated the man who'd had Hankins covered with his own drawn pistol. Grady was confused because the man was suddenly being very friendly.

Aires noticed Grady's confusion and smiled, "I'm sorry we barged in here like bears and pushed your people around, but we had to test you. You passed by the way."

Grady's anger returned, "You tested me? Why? How? I..."

Director Aires held up his hand, good-naturedly and said, "Look I've found that, normally, a man with something to hide will put up with just about anything from us to keep on our good side, until he learns what we know. A man with nothing to hide, usually acts like you did, except that I must say, yours was the most violent reaction I've ever seen!"

"I'm Irish, with a full helping of the Irish temper

and I don't like my people being pushed around! I don't do it and I won't let others!"

Grady tried to calm down.

He took a deep breath and said, "My Irish temper does get the best of me from time to time. Now that we're all civilized again, could you please explain to me what's going on?"

Aires turned to Swaggert, and said, "The file please, Bob."

"Mr. Director, I still object to bringing the Chief into this. This is classified information!"

The director held out his hand, and said, "Objection noted, but it is my call."

Bob handed the file over to the director, who in turn handed it to Grady. Grady looked at the cover and saw the large red print "TOP SECRET", which was sprawled across it. He looked up at the director who nodded. Grady broke the seal and opened the file. On the first page was a picture of a rough looking character. He was dressed in a black jump suit. The notes indicated he was six feet one inch tall and looked to have a lean muscular build. His nose looked crooked, like it'd been broken once too often. There was a nasty scar that traveled from the man's left temple, across his left eye, nose and ended on his right cheek. It was a jagged rough scar, which looked as though it'd healed without the benefit of the stitches it'd obviously needed! He had black hair, which was cut in a "Crew-cut" style. All in all he looked mean!

Beneath the picture was stated the following facts, which Grady read out loud, "Starvas Creen, Cleansing

Unit Leader, division one, unit one.   Rank: Captain.
Clearance: Optimum.   Warning: Unstable personality.
Additional Warning: Vanished Renegade.   Believed to
work for Committee."

Grady looked up at the director, and said, "Starvas
Creen?   A report was just filed against this man for
conspiracy to commit murder, intimidation and blackmail!"

The director looked at his men, then sat forward on
the edge of his seat and whispered, "He's here, in
Covenant?"

Grady also sat forward, "No, he's not, but he sent a
man, named Sam Crawford, here to kill Rev. Smith in
exchange for dropping the man's gambling debt; but Mr.
Crawford had a change of heart and turned States
evidence against Creen.   By the way, how do you lose an
operative and what is the Committee?"

The director turned to Special Agent Jones and
said, "Would you field this one, George?"

"Yes sir! Creen was one of my best agents. He was
ruthless, effective and reliable, that is, until he got
hooked up with the committee! The committee is made
up of twelve very powerful people from around the world.
They're always interfering with our plans in order to
advance their own agenda, which is to create a One World
Government, and through it control the world! Until a
few days ago, we couldn't figure out why he'd defect to
their cause; with us, he had all a man could ever want. It
wasn't until Joshua White turned up missing that we
understood!"

Grady waited for more, but Jones stopped and
looked at the director, who nodded.

He continued, as he reached over and removed the first page uncovering the second, "As you can see from this picture, your friend, Joshua White, was once a member of Creen's elite cleansing unit."

Grady looked at a very young Joshua White dressed in that same black jump suit and same close-cropped hair.

Grady read, "Joshua White, Cleansing Unit One, second in command, Division one. Rank: Lieutenant. Clearance: level one. Caution: Christian beliefs limit his usefulness."

Grady looked at the director, "He gave you guys trouble even back then?"

The director took over, "Yes, Chief. There was a hearing after an incident on one of their more delicate operations. White and Creen were to assassinate a certain government leader. When they were in position, White found the man's entire family was in the house they were about to blow so he tried to defuse the bomb. Creen attacked him and the fight was on. I'm sure you noticed the broken nose and scar on Creen's face?"

Grady nodded.

"Well, White did that during their fight! It was reported to be one violent battle! A battle between Creen, who was the best, and White, who took him, causing Creen to lose face in more ways than one! Creen vowed to get even with Joshua White one day. Well, we feel that the day has arrived!"

Grady said, "How so?"

Jones spoke up, "We've just learned that Creen was responsible for abducting Joshua White and President Place."

Grady jumped up, "What do you mean President Place!"

Jones stated, as calmly as if he were describing the outcome of a game of chess, "President Place was abducted the same night as Joshua White along with her son and doctor. They're all missing!"

Grady thought of Josh's dream and said, "Josh had a dream about the enemy attacking the White House. He was warned but didn't understand!"

It was the director's turn to jump up and ask, "What enemy is that Chief?"

Grady hesitated, shrugged and said, "An evil demon has been attacking Covenant for a couple of years now. There's more at work here than you know director!"

The director sighed with relief and said, "I can't worry about ghosts and demons. I have a country to protect. . ."

Grady interrupted, "Director, I know it sounds like make believe but trust me, it's true! There are evil, supernatural forces at work behind this committee of yours. We need to fight them at all levels!"

The director smiled, "Fine! You attack the demons, but I need your help to attack the men involved. We'll be calling on you and your entire force very shortly to capture some criminals. Are you up to it?" He looked at Grady's arm as he said this last.

Grady said, "Yes, I'm up to anything that'll help get Josh back. Director, you still haven't explained what all of this has to do with the agents that my men and I had to shoot."

There was a knock on the door. Grady motioned and Hankins entered with a pot of coffee and three mugs.

"Thanks Jimmy. Look, tell the guys they can go back out on patrol, everything's cool."

Jimmy Hankins nodded but he still looked suspicious as he left.

Grady got up, poured coffee all around and said, "I have good officers. They're very loyal!"

The Director whispered, almost under his breath, "They'll have to be!"

The men were silent for a few moments as they sipped their coffee and gathered their thoughts.

Grady finally said, "Now director, what does this have to do with your two agents?"

The director said, "Chief, everything we've told you and everything we're about to tell you is classified, therefore, must be kept between us. Agreed?"

Grady nodded.

The director continued, "These two men were part of Creen's Cleansing unit. You see when he left, his entire unit left with him. They're also very loyal! We feel they were sent here to kill you and Marla Brinkle, your fiancée I believe? You're very lucky to be alive, because these two men never miss a target. To tell you the truth, I'm impressed that you and your men were able to stop them at all! They were very good at their jobs."

Grady's head was spinning. First, he was relieved that he and Marla were alive, but he was also angry that the dead men had endangered Marla.

Then he thought about Joshua, *"No wonder he could fight so well and always seemed so cool and collected. He was a secret agent of sorts!"*

Grady looked at the director and said, "Could I

suggest that we get some rest and reconvene in the morning?"

The director said, "Yes, that would be acceptable, say eight in the morning?"

"Yes, I'll have some breakfast sent over if you like and we can talk over a nice meal?"

The director nodded, shook Grady's left hand and the three men left his office.

Grady left the office without telling his people anything. He drove home, took a shower and finally got the rest he so badly needed.

Director Aires needed a walk! He turned to Agents Swaggert and Jones and said, "I need to get some air and think. You go ahead, have supper, get some drinks and I'll meet you in the lounge of the motel."

Bob, forever the cautious one, asked, "Are you sure it's wise to be walking around alone under the circumstances?"

The director smiled and replied, "Thanks for the concern Bob, but I can take care of myself. I don't think Creen, or any of his ghouls, will be lurking about in the middle of the city."

The two men reluctantly agreed, turned toward the car and headed for much anticipated drinks.

The Director walked out of the parking lot, turned the collar of his topcoat up to protect his neck from the chill night air and headed in the general direction of the motel, three miles away.

The only sounds were the occasional barking of dogs or the hiss and scream of fighting tomcats in one alley or another. The director watched as the wind swirled the dry leaves down the sidewalk causing the forming fog to part for their passage.

Suddenly, he felt cold and alone. The responsibilities he carried were heavy, dangerous and very demanding.

He thought, "*Richard Aires, Director of the CIA. How I longed for that title! How I've fought for position, out maneuvering my competition at every turn, bending the rules and even covering up for one politician or another when they* **were** *caught breaking the law or performing immoral acts. But now, God, if there be a God, I'm tired! I'm tired of all of the corruption, the deceit, the back-stabbing and the violence. I long for entire days of rest, with no responsibilities, dangers or fears to haunt me. I long for this present adventure to be over...*"

The director snapped out of his reverie when he sensed the danger. He'd absentmindedly listened to his own echoing footsteps clip-clopping along the sidewalk at a slow methodical pace. His years of training and field experience told him that someone was hiding up ahead of him in the alley. He no longer could tell if it was a sound, a smell, the movement of a shadow out of place or perhaps it was just a sixth sense that had alerted him, but whatever it was, he knew beyond a shadow of doubt that there was danger ahead!

He instinctively pulled his gun and held it down to his side, keeping his pace the same, as he walked closer to the entrance of the alley.

When he arrived at the alley's entrance, he turned suddenly, raised his gun, pointing it at the shadowy unrecognizable figure in the fog and said, "Step out here where I can see you!"

The shadow replied, "I see you haven't lost you skills, Director."

Director Aires recognized that voice and he relaxed somewhat. The figure moved and suddenly Spike, a.k.a. Jarrett White, a.k.a. Eagle and undercover CIA agent, was standing before the Director.

The two men hugged in greeting then the Director said, "You look tired my friend."

"That I am Richard! It's been a long couple of years but it's about to pay off! I've collected about fifty of the most notorious and dangerous men I could find and I can't wait to get them off of my hands. Will tomorrow night work for you Director?"

"That's fine with me. What do you have in mind?"

"I've been watching the local police and I believe they can help us."

"I agree, Jarrett. They killed Andy and Leon, you know."

"Yes, I saw them in action and they're quite good. Now here's what I have in mind. Tomorrow night around 7:00, I'll direct my men to rob these specific stores."

He pulled out a map of the city that had certain sites marked in red. He turned on his red-tinted night light and said, as he illuminated the map, "Here's what you do Director! Place men here, here and here..."

Unseen by man or beast in the fog-engulfed alley around them, the Director and Special Agent Jarrett White made their plans for the capture of the **Demon Slayers**.

CHAPTER SEVENTEEN
A MATTER OF TERRITORY

Capt. Rumpus was terrified! He'd stupidly over stepped his authority this time. His thoughts were racing twice as fast as his body. He was flying toward Tumult's stronghold, approaching a meeting that he dreaded immensely.

"How was I to know that this upstart Tumult would be given such high authority by the Lord Satan?"

Once he found out he had, of course, tried to make it up to Lt. Crygen hoping that he wouldn't tell Tumult. Just one day after he left, however, Rumpus received a summons to appear before Tumult.

"It galls me to have to grovel to this failure Tumult. It wasn't fair that Satan gave him all this power after his failure at the Battle of Covenant! I should've gotten this assignment, myself, but now I'm just an errand boy!"

Capt. Rumpus cut his thoughts short, as he landed in front of Tumult's stronghold. He raised his knobby right hand and pounded on the large wooden doors of the chamber with much more confidence than he felt.

When there was no answer, he found himself stupidly hoping that no one was home. His hopes were dashed, however, when the massive doors separated, squeaking on their rusty hinges. Inside the doors was a vast chamber and a horde of waiting demons.

"Not a good sign!" thought Rumpus.

At the far end of the chamber, sitting high on his

throne, was Tumult, currently second in command to Satan himself.

Tumult smiled down on Rumpus and bellowed across the chamber, his booming bass voice echoing off of the walls bringing silence to the crowd.

"Come in! Come in, Rumpus, my friend!"

Rumpus nervously thought, *"No, not a good sign at all!"*

He started walking slowly toward Tumult looking all around him as he did. The now silent demons all smiled down at him with an expression, which said, "We'll enjoy watching Tumult dissect you alive!"

Tumult began the descent from his lofty throne and arrived at the bottom of the stairs at the same time as Rumpus. Tumult's long cape was dragging on the stairs and the crown he wore was slightly cocked on his head. He seemed to be in a very jovial mood and, this too, made Rumpus very nervous! Very nervous indeed! He began to perspire.

Tumult slapped Rumpus on the back and said as he led him toward a large table, "My friend, how have you been? I've been hearing some good things about you, but I've also heard a couple of disturbing things as well!"

Fear twisted Rumpus's heart, formed a lump in his throat and a knot in his stomach, but he remained silent continuing toward the massive table in the middle of the room.

Tumult continued, "You're so quiet, my friend," he slapped Rumpus on the back good-naturedly and shouted, "Come on lighten up; it won't be that bad!"

With that, Tumult raised his gnarled right hand, an unseen force picked Rumpus up and threw him onto the table face down. He was held tight by invisible bonds and he watched helplessly as Lt. Crygen came out of a side room carrying a wicked looking whip.

Rumpus sighed with relief, thinking, *"I'm to be beaten then, not killed!"*

Crygen reared back and threw all of his weight into the first blow. The sixteen leather straps laced with bones ripped into Rumpus' back. The crowd of demons cheered wildly. Rumpus counted twenty blows before he lost consciousness. His last thought was, *"Perhaps I'm to be beaten to death after all!"*

His hearing came back first, as he made out casual conversation all around him. He stirred and found that his arms and legs were now free so he rolled over. That was a mistake; he slipped off the edge of the table and fell onto the floor directly onto his shredded back. His screams of pain focused the attention of the crowd back to him and demons all around him howled with laughter. Rumpus was humiliated and felt his face turn red with shame. As he rose to his feet, he heard Tumult's booming voice again.

"Ahhh! Rumpus you're back with us, I see. Come over here my faithful servant and bow before your master!"

Laughter came from all sides. Rumpus was dizzy and could barely focus on Tumult who was sitting on his throne once again. Rumpus stumbled up the mountain of stairs and fell prostrate before Tumult and said, "My Lord! Forgive me my transgressions! I didn't know that you held this office, or I would've been more respectful to Lt. Crygen!"

Tumult bent down and helped Rumpus to his feet

by pulling on a loose flap of torn flesh. He spoke, "Rise Captain, no harm done. Luckily for you Lt. Crygen is more forgiving than I. Had you treated me like that, I would've slit your throat, but consider yourself forgiven!"

With that, he slapped Rumpus on the back renewing the spasm of pain that had racked his back and caused him to cry out, to the delight of all the assembled demons.

Tumult started down the stairs, saying, "Come, let's eat!"

Rumpus took a step to follow him, but in his dizzy weakened condition lost his footing and fell. Tumult jumped allowing Rumpus to roll under him down the entire flight of stairs. Pain exploded in Rumpus' back as he struck each step.

He laughed as he reached the bottom and bent to help the pitiful Rumpus to his feet again, "Rumpus, you're much more humorous than I gave you credit for! Come! Eat! Get your strength back and then we'll talk."

Rumpus allowed himself to be led toward the feast, but his thoughts were on revenge not food! He ate in painful silence, savoring his thoughts of vindication as a smile slowly appeared on his tortured features.

*   *   *

Grady and Director Aires grabbed for the last piece of pizza. Grady victoriously took a bite while the Director frowned in defeat. Director Aires picked up the maps and started to summarize the plans that they'd been reviewing all morning.

"I think this'll be a very workable plan, Chief; we'll have our men here and in place on time."

Grady put the last of the pizza in his mouth mumbling between bites, "I have to ask you, Dick, how do you know everything you know? For instance, how can you possibly know with such certainty who took Josh and President Place? How can you know where they're being held? Most especially how can you know what's about to happen to this city?"

The Director smiled and said, "All right Chief, even though you stole my piece of pizza this afternoon and the last sausage this morning, I'll tell you everything. You have to understand, however, that you can't tell anyone what I've shared with you. No one at all, do you understand?"

Grady, familiar with this qualifying statement, replied impatiently, "Yes! Yes! I've said three hundred times that I won't tell a soul and I won't."

The two men, with the Director, sighed and shook their heads in unison, as if the disclosure of each secret he told Grady was ripping their hearts from their chests.

"Over the last few years, we've managed to get two of our best agents deep under cover. Their code names are Eagle and Hawk. Eagle paid me a visit last night."

This got everyone's attention as the Director continued, "I must withhold their true names, but they've worked their way deep into the Committee's operation and at great personal risk and sacrifice I might add. They're now in good positions to keep us informed. It seems that the Committee was responsible for the attempted assassination of your friend Joshua White two years ago. When that failed and their pawn Governor

Bradley killed himself, they decided to bring White directly to the Committee and handle things themselves. They've now made their move.

"Our moles have reported that White and the President have stepped on the Committee's toes with their Christian teachings and efforts to turn America back to its Christian heritage. They don't want things returning to God's rule. On the contrary, they've been working very hard over the years to wipe out Christianity all together!

"This gives us their motivation, but we still don't know what they hope to accomplish, unless they just plan to cut off the head and hope the body dies."

Grady wiped his mouth on a napkin and said, "It's been that way all through history. They killed Jesus hoping to have that very effect, but the opposite happened. You'd think that the enemy would learn by now wouldn't you?"

The Director said, "In her first term as President, Roberta Place has made abortion illegal again. She's put prayer back into the schools, government meetings and public places. The Ten Commandments are back on walls where they once hung. She stopped the attempt to take "In God We Trust", off of the US currency. She also has made all drugs illegal, including marijuana and has stepped up our efforts to prevent the import of these drugs from other countries. It had been our job, in the CIA, to help bring these drugs into the country in order to help the economy of the Third World countries that provided them. President Place stopped that practice. "What's really gotten the Committee angry, however, is the fact that President Place is beginning to limit the US involvement in the UN. She's backing off of her former position of bringing about a One World Order under the authority of the U.N. President Place feels that the world has a better chance, if the United States keeps its own government under its original Constitution and not under the newly proposed UN Constitution, which would take away US sovereignty. Because of these and numerous other issues, there are certain people who don't want President Place to be re-elected next month!"

"Director, I was wondering, how did they get to the President? I thought her security was fool proof!"

The Director blushed, "So did we, but we now feel that the Committee has someone working on the inside of the White House. Someone high up. As a matter of fact, we think it may be Vice President Huggens."

Swaggert and Jones ran their hands through their hair and whispered, "We give up!" They weren't as accustomed to briefing outsiders as the Director.

Aires smiled as he continued, "When we questioned him, he played a tape that had the President saying she was sick, needed time alone and Huggens was in charge. We don't know how he got the tape, but we know President Place wouldn't leave Huggens in charge of mopping her floor. We have agents watching his every move and we'll nail him as soon as he slips up!"

Grady said, "Thanks for your candor in these matters, Richard. I think if all the different departments would cooperate like this instead of keeping secrets from each other more could be accomplished.

"Well, I better get going if I'm to get all the plans in place by tonight. I also have to get Marla and her news team lined up for tonight's special prayer meeting, which is being broadcast worldwide. They'll get the world to pray for the enemies who've taken Joshua. I won't mention that the President is also missing, but it's the same enemy so it won't matter. I know you don't think that prayers help all that much, but Rev. Smith assures me it'll deal guite a blow to the demon world."

The meeting broke up and they all went their own way to prepare for the night's activities.

*   *   *

The meal was actually pretty good. Rumpus would've enjoyed it better without the pain of loose teeth, but at least he was alive! He knew that one day he'd turn this around on Tumult. One day, he'd be on top and he'd make Tumult pay for this insult. Until that time, however, he'd be friendly and cooperative with his new master.

As Tumult sat back and wiped his mouth on his sleeve, he said, "Now, Rumpus, let's get down to business shall we. What progress have you made?"

Rumpus bowed slightly, and then reported, "As you know sir, I was given charge of the Committee at its inception, over two hundred years ago. With patience and cunning we've brought about the dilution of Christianity here in the States. We allowed the Christians to start this country, but then slowly we diluted their morality, their focus and their purpose. We've influenced the humans through drugs, sex and violence. We've dehumanized them and made them like animals in their relations with each other. Most importantly we've made them believe the spiritual world is a myth; that it doesn't exist!

"Even when this upstart White and President Place turned on us and started to reverse all of our work, we didn't give up. We went out, captured them and are in the process, even as we speak, of brainwashing them to turn them to our purpose. Once they're beaten and shocked into compliance, we'll finish destroying the American family unit, which will finish the country once and for all. We'll then get our people to do away with the Constitution and allow the US to take its place in the One World Order. Then all will be in readiness for Satan to come and take over His world!"

Tumult liked what he'd just heard and only had to figure out how to get Rumpus to do all the work, but to have all the credit for himself.

Tumult said, "Well done Rumpus! You have my full confidence. I'm counting on you to make sure all of these things come to pass. As for the President and this White...kill them! Kill them now!"

CHAPTER EIGHTEEN
SPIKE-NAILED

Carrying a supper tray, Angela walked into Dr. Kamerman's office. She found him pacing back and forth. His face appeared to have more wrinkles than she remembered and his hair was a bit grayer. His hair, which was normally very neat and in place, was standing straight out in all direction like he'd been running his hands through it and then pulling on it. The doctor looked in her direction and relaxed somewhat. It was all Angela could do not to laugh at the sight, but she maintained her zombie-like appearance.

Dr. Kamerman had skipped lunch and it was already past six. Seeing Angela with the tray of food reminded him how hungry he was, but he had to find out something before he could eat. He ran over to Angela grabbed her arms and shook her almost upsetting the tray in the process.

He shouted, "Angela, do I look insane to you?"

To Angela, he looked like a little boy who was afraid of how a new pimple made him look. She smiled on the outside but was laughing uncontrollably on the inside. She put the tray down on the doctor's desk and took his hand. She walked over to his large armchair and sat down pulling him onto her lap. She pulled his head down to her shoulder; he left it there and wept for quite awhile.

As Angela held him to her chest, rocking back and forth, stroking his hair gently and humming to him softly, her eyes were scanning the monitors behind his desk.

189

She saw that Joshua and President Place were together and they were safe. They were holding hands facing each other, heads bowed while praying. Unseen by the weeping doctor, Angela smiled as she continued to gently stroke the back of his head.

She thought, *"It won't be long now doctor before I rip your evil heart from your body."*

*   *   *

This evening, Winter, Spike's second in command seemed somewhat nervous. Spike watched him cautiously.

He finally asked, "Winter, what's the matter with you tonight. You're more jumpy than a long-tailed cat in a room full of rocking chairs!"

Winter smiled weakly and said, "I don't know Spike! I just have a bad feeling about tonight. Sister Gen did a reading for me earlier saying there's deception and capture on the horizon."

Spike jumped to his feet and yelled, "Are you suggesting that one of my men would dare to betray me!"

Winter swallowed hard and said, "No Spike! I don't know, I just feel nervous about tonight's operation!"

Spike spoke more softly, "Well, Sister Gen's just a little nervous herself about a warning given to her by her Spirit Guide.

"Just forget all of this hocus-pocus and go forth to rob, destroy and intimidate; the three things that we do best! Remember though, no cop killing. I don't want them looking too intensely for us; not yet anyway!"

Winter nodded and Spike continued, "Just

remember our objective is to have Covenant feel our sting, but not leave a clue as to where the sting came from! You'll hit only the businesses that I've outlined. Don't deviate from the plan at all! Do you understand?"

Winter nodded again as Spike finished his instructions, "Also, leave your bikes hidden outside of town and walk in. Strike hard and fast, then get back here. You have one hour starting now, to get into position."

They compared watches, shook hands and Winter left to gather the men. They'd strike at 7:00 exactly.

*   *   *

Sore, humiliated and in a foul mood Rumpus returned to his chamber only to find Dr. Kamerman sitting in Angela's lap weeping! Rumpus looked at the sleeping demon that he'd left in charge of the doctor and rage filled his eyes. He pulled his sword, screamed at the top of his lungs and attacked the guard. The small demon didn't even have time to protest as the blade passed through his neck severing his head from his body. There was a small puff of sulfuric smoke and he was gone.

Pouncing on the doctor's chest Rumpus dug his yellow-clawed gnarled left hand into the doctor's heart, sunk his right claw deep into the doctor's spine and yelled into his soul, "Kill them! Kill them! Kill them now!"

The doctor's headache, which had been easing, came back with a vengeance. He jumped up, startling Angela, and began to chant, "Kill them! Kill them! Kill them now!"

Angela could see he'd totally lost his mind! He was

quite mad! Trying to calm him and divert his attention, Angela walked over to his desk, picked up the tray and said, "Doctor why don't you sit down and eat your nice dinner?"

He looked at her with unseeing, panic stricken eyes. As a matter of fact, she could swear that they had a reddish glow to them. Without warning, he ran over to her, flung the tray of food across the room and punched Angela square on the jaw. She was flung backward over the desk and landed on her back. She shook her head, leaned on her right elbow, wiped the blood away from her mouth with her left hand and watched the doctor who was walking in circles chanting the same words over and over.

Finally, he shrieked at her as he stormed out of the room, "Get this mess cleaned up! I'll deal with you later!"

*   *   *

Joshua could feel the power of the Holy Spirit filling his soul as he and the President prayed. Both Christians were in awe of the power they were experiencing! They were praying for their enemies and felt genuine forgiveness for them deep in their souls. They'd been praying in the Spirit for hours but it seemed mere minutes.

Vaguely aware that their cell door was opening, Joshua glanced in that direction, then tensed dropping the President's hands. He was staring into the sneering face of Starvas Creen.

The smug look on his face told Joshua that the time had finally come. They were to be killed and Starvas was going to enjoy it!

Starvas said, "Well Josh, we finally meet face to face. I've been waiting for years for this little treat! I would've preferred to beat you to death with my own bare hands," he shrugged his shoulders, "but I've got my orders."

The doctor came running in. He had the look of a wild man.

He screamed, "Don't talk to them! Kill them! Kill them now!"

Starvas Creen with a pained look on his face said, "Look what I've come to, Joshua. I'm working for a mad man, but he does pay well. Oh well, it was nice getting to abduct you and the President, and now I've got the pleasure of killing you both myself!"

He raised his 9mm while Joshua and the President knelt once more and prayed.

Suddenly two shots rang out and Starvas Creen fell face forward to the ground.

Angela came in brandishing a .38 caliber snub nose. Doctor Kamerman looked shocked and for a moment just stared at her in disbelief.

He finally said, "Angela what..."

Angela yelled, "Shut up you fool! Don't say anything to me or I'll kill you where you stand!"

Angela had come into the cell and now stood between the doctor and the prisoners. Suddenly the doctor ran for the door. Angela shot once. The bullet just missed the doctor's head. She fired again and the bullet slammed into the doctor's right arm knocking him down. With speed that even surprised the doctor, he jumped up and hit the emergency override. A steel plate fell over the door sealing the doctor out and them in the cell.

Joshua and the President had watched this unexpected turn of events from their position on the floor. They watched dumbfounded as the woman turned and pointed the .38 at Joshua. He knew from experience that this type of pistol held five shots, that the last of the live rounds was in the chamber and was now pointed at his head. He once again called on his Lord for help.

*   *   *

Spike was sitting at the table with Sister Gen. She was laying her Tarot cards out before them desperately trying to get some good news for a change, but her Spirit Guide was full of nothing but gloom.

Sister Gen said, "I'm worried Spike. First, we're warned to stay away from Covenant and now these cards say that there's a shadow of betrayal around you."

Spike jumped up, knocked the cards off of the table and pulled his knife, yelling, "I'm getting tired of being told that my men will betray me."

Before Sister Gen could answer, the door to the trailer burst open and several men dressed in black yelled at the same time, "Police! Drop that knife! Get down on the floor! Hurry up! Down on your face!"

Sister Gen screamed but complied. Spike dropped the knife and thought about going for his gun, but held his hand. Instead, he lay down on his face in order to cover the smile that was forming there.

*   *   *

Far above them Andy drew his sword and attacked

Aliron. He'd been assigned to protect Jarrett White and that's exactly what he was going to do! The first order of business, however, was to get rid of Sister Gen's demon. He didn't want any undue influence on Jarrett later.

After several thrusts and parries Aliron could see Andy's determination. Aliron fled with a scream of fear. Andy drew his dagger and threw it at the fleeing Aliron who swiftly dissolved into a puff of putrid smoke. Andy then flew down to protect his new charge who at this very moment was being loaded into a police car. He'd be driven to Covenant and the new way of life on which he was about to embark!

CHAPTER NINETEEN
BUSTED AND BUSTING OUT

Marla Brinkle and her news staff had been working all day setting up for the televised prayer meeting. Marla had called in many favors to get the required permission. The station owners were crying about ratings, and she had put her neck and her career on the chopping block by promising them excellent results from this telecast.

"Lord, please don't let me down!", she prayed as they finished the last of the arrangements and Debbie called her into makeup. Marla ran over and sat down looking at her watch as she did so.

She told Debbie, "I'm sorry it took so long. I've only left you thirty minutes to make me beautiful!"

Debbie smiled and said, "Well, this is supposed to be the place for miracles isn't it?"

They laughed and Marla's stomach calmed a bit.

Marla's thoughts turned to the fact that this would be the first attempt to get the world to pray for someone's enemy and she was hoping that it would work!

*   *   *

Hankins looked at his watch, 6:59 and 45 seconds, any second now. He'd deployed his men as Chief O'Leary had instructed him. He'd only been told that a massive robbery was about to take place, and he and his men were responsible for apprehending the suspects. He'd also been told the suspects would be heavily armed and very dangerous. Hankins whispered into his radio and heard their voices in his earplug as all stations checked in. Everyone was ready, coiled as tightly as over wound watch springs!

The first sound he heard was the scuffing of a shoe against stone. Next, he heard a whispered curse as the man ran into a garbage can and then he saw the shadow of two men as they approached the back of the drug store. He watched as they broke the light over the door and picked the lock. They entered swiftly and expertly. Hankins moved up quietly and was in position when the men emerged. They didn't notice him as they walked right past his position behind the store's dumpster. Hankins aimed and shouted, "Freeze police!"

One of the men turned to fire his weapon and Hankins shot him in the face. The other man struck like a snake, jumping Hankins before he could swing his gun around to him.

When Hankins hit the ground, the gun fell from his hand and he just barely caught the man's wrist before the sharp point of his knife pierced his face. Hankins was using both of his hands to hold the knife back but was still losing the battle, for the knife was inching closer!

He yelled through grunts of effort, "Give it up man! Don't add to your crimes!"

The man screamed back, "Not until I kill you, fool! You shot one of my men and for that you must die!"

Hankins took his right hand away and quickly dug in the right breast pocket of his jump suit and felt the field knife resting there. The blade had a large circle-shaped hole in it that allowed Hankins to open the folded blade with one hand. He hesitated not wanting to stab another human being but at that moment his attacker's blade pierced the skin of his forehead and began cutting it's way down toward his right eye. Hankins closed his eyes and thrust the blade deep into the man's neck. He felt the blade cut through muscles and tendons. He felt the man's warm, life giving blood as it poured from his neck and onto Hankins' face. Finally, he felt the man tense and then go limp.

It took all the strength Hankins had left to slip out from under the other's deadly blade. He lay on his back trembling from the effort and emotion of their encounter. As he lay there, he heard other officers yelling warnings, occasional gunfire and a lot of yelling and cursing. Hankins knew he'd never forget the sights, sounds and smells of this night. Never!

*   *   *

Marla's engineer counted down three, two, one. He pointed.

"This is Marla Brinkle reporting live from Jesus Park, located just outside the city of Covenant. We're here tonight, with not only news, but with a request! Standing here with me is Rev. Smith, the Director of Jesus Park, to explain. Rev. Smith."

"Thank you, Marla. It's a pleasure to have people from all over the world join us here tonight. There've been thousands of miracles performed by the Lord at Jesus Park and we want to share these experiences with your entire TV audience! We also, as you said, have a request this evening.

"A wise woman named Granny Girard gave us a

message as she lay dying. She convinced us that the best way to defeat Satan is to pray for our enemies! Jesus also told us, 'pray for those who persecute you and do all kinds of evil against you'. Now we're asking our listening audience to join with us as we do just that! We want to pray for the men responsible for abducting Joshua White, whom as you know is our founder and we believe, a modern prophet for Jesus. If you'll allow me, Marla, I'll go up to the microphone and get my audience ready as you prepare your own audience."

"Thank you, Rev. Smith."

Marla turned again toward the camera and continued, "As you know, we've reported the disappearance of Joshua White, founder and benefactor of Jesus Park. It's believed that he's been abducted by unknown opponents for unknown reasons, but...

"Excuse me, but here comes Ellen White, Joshua's fiancée."

Marla looked away for a moment and shouted, "Ellen! Yes, Ellen, over here!"

Ellen came nervously into the picture and Marla said, "I know this is a trying time for you, Ellen but we need to hear from you. I want you to tell the viewing audience what happened to you the other night."

Ellen cleared her throat and tears began to swell in her eyes.

She said, "Well, Marla, as I told you, they came in like ghosts. They hit hard and fast! They were all dressed in black and they beat me up and took Joshua away!"

"They did this to you?", Marla pointed at Ellen's black eye.

"Yes, they hit me with their guns."

"Thank you Ellen. We'll let you get up to the stage, I believe Rev. Smith is ready to begin the prayer service." Marla turned her attention to the stage where Rev. Smith was leading the opening prayer.

In homes all over America and in many more homes throughout the world via satellite, people began to pray for the enemies who'd taken Joshua and messed up his life so badly.

*   *   *

As Joshua prayed, he kept his eyes on the woman's gun. She hadn't said anything as if she were thinking, trying to make a decision.

Suddenly Starvas Creen jumped up and ran toward the woman. His bulletproof vest had stopped the bullets. He'd simply been knocked out when his head hit the floor.

Before Joshua could get off of his knees, the frail looking woman kicked back causing Creen's knee to snap with an audible "crack". He fell near to his 9mm and grabbed for it. As he reached out with his right hand the woman shot her final shot, which pierced Creen's hand dead center.

He screamed, "Who are you?! Why are you doing this? Why are you helping these Christians?"

The woman said sarcastically, "My, my, aren't we just full of questions today, Creen. Now you just lie there and I'll explain everything to you all."

She turned a little more toward Joshua and the President but kept her eyes on Creen as she bent down and picked up his 9 mm. She stepped back out of his reach and began her story.

"My name is Angela Boner. I work for CIA Director Aires. I came here a little over a year ago as a deep under cover operative to spy on Dr. Kamerman's operation. I can't even begin to tell you the things that man's done to me, but I wish it were he on the floor, Creen, instead of you! It would appear that my job here is finished, except for getting you two out."

Angela took a small black box out of her pants pocket and said, "We need to stop by and pick up your son and your doctor Madam President.

President Place jumped up and for the first time since this began, she spoke, "What do you mean?"

Angela smiled, "I mean that they arrived here the same night you did. Don't worry though, they're together and haven't been harmed in anyway."

A hissing sound permeated the cell.

"Knock-out gas!", Angela yelled, "Let's get out of here!" With that she pushed a button on the remote and the steel plate over the door rose into the ceiling once again. Angela ran out into the hall and saw that it was clear. She turned back to hurry the two captives up but they were gone. After checking the cell again and giving Creen one final kick in the face, Angela left, pushed the button on the remote and allowed the steel plate to drop into place once more. The hair on the back of her neck stood on end as she tried to think about what had just occurred.

"Where did Joshua and President Place go?", she whispered as she scratched her head.

*   *   *

Dr. Kamerman sat in his office and watched his monitors. He saw to his great surprise how effectively Angela had taken care of Creen. He'd heard her explanation of whom she was and his anger grew.

He reached out and released the knock-out gas. He'd knock them out, then re-secure them all! He'd personally take great pleasure in dissecting Angela's live body! The doctor watched with growing surprise and concern as Angela took out the remote to effect their release, but what he saw next threatened to drive him beyond sanity forever!

As Joshua White and the President started toward the exit, two angels appeared behind them as if out of nowhere. They laid a hand on the shoulder of each human, then they all disappeared as if they'd never been there at all! Dr. Kamerman decided that it was time to retreat and regroup later. He pushed another button and as the chair in which he sat lowered him into the depths below, he began to laugh. It was the eerie laugh of a man lost in madness!

CHAPTER TWENTY
SCOOP OF THE YEAR

Tumult was in his throne room when it hit. At first, the chamber just vibrated with a low frequency hum. Then the walls of the chamber began to crack, causing smaller pieces of rock to fall to the floor below. Demons began to scream in pain and hold their ears, as the rumble grew louder. Tumult stared as the doors to his chamber exploded, splintering into a million shards of wood. He strained to see through the dust and the light that came from beyond the door. Gradually as the air cleared, he saw a figure standing silhouetted in the doorway. The figure pulled his sword, and the chamber was lit as by the noonday sun. There in the doorway stood Capt. Worl, the angel in charge of the United States of America.

The shadows of the frenzied demons danced like wraiths against the chamber walls. Worl stepped aside and the brilliance grew as a legion of angels filled the chamber, and the war began. Worl shouted over the turmoil, "Tumult, your day has arrived. I'll send you back to Hell again and this time you'll not escape the attention of your master so quickly, I'll wager!"

Tumult shrieked in reply, "I've already destroyed your precious Joshua White and President Place! They'll not trouble my kingdom again!"

Worl smiled, "Wrong again, Tumult! We've rescued them and they're safely away from your human hosts. As a matter of fact, you've also lost Jarrett White to our side!

I have ten angels guarding him as we speak and he'll remain unapproachable to your side until he has a chance to grow in his new faith! What will your lord Satan have to say about that, Tumult?"

Tumult threw his crown at Worl, drew his sword and bellowed in rage as he flew toward him.

In his anger, Tumult was very careless and just barreled toward his target with no plan or thought in his evil head.

Worl stood his ground until the very last moment and then turned to the right. Tumult flew past him and as Worl completed his turn, his sword severed the head of the mighty Tumult. But even after his head rolled to the floor, his body continued on until it hit the far wall. Then both his head and body disappeared in a puff of yellowish, brown smoke.

Worl held his sword high and gave the victory shout. One angel after another joined him until there were no demons left to fight and only the angels were left to celebrate. With a hand signal from Worl, all the angels left the chamber. Just as Worl dissolved, he snapped his fingers, causing Tumult's former chamber, once a seat of great power, to dissolve into millions of dust particles which were then scattered to all corners of the earth as a warning to other demons.

Tumult wasn't the only demon having trouble this night! The Christian's massive worldwide prayer service also attacked Rumpus, who barely saved his own life by possessing Dr. Kamerman and driving him far underground. Lt. Crygen possessed Starvas Creen and in so doing saved himself from sure destruction. Over three million of their demon cohorts weren't so lucky however.

The demon world was shaken to its very foundation and Satan, Himself, writhed in pain as the prayers of the Saints reached His domain!

Satan bellowed, "Tumuuult! I want Tumuuult!"

At that very moment Tumult appeared before his lord Satan carrying his own head.

Satan's entire being was engulfed in pain and his thoughts were filled with the blackness of pure hatred for Tumult and his failures. Tumult saw the look in Satan's eyes as his lord left his throne and started walking down the steps toward him; slowly at first then faster as the intensity of his anger flared. The eyes in Tumult's severed head looked right and then left, frantically trying to find a place to hide from Satan's wrath. In one last desperate attempt to escape, Tumult threw his severed head at Satan and his body ran in the opposite direction. Satan caught Tumult's head, bit Tumult's nose off and while chewing it with satisfaction, threw the remainder of Tumult's head at his fleeing body. It hit the demon between the shoulder blades causing him to career out of control and fall to the floor.

The Father of Lies was on him in seconds and when he had finally taken every last ounce of anger out on Tumult, he demoted what was left of him to the lowest, least important tar pit in the Nether World. He would crawl in the slime there for eternity, fighting pitifully for any crumb of dignity that he might find.

Satan smiled and thought, '*A fitting end to yet another failure.*'

He wiped Tumult's blood from his hands as he ascended the stairs to his throne and by the time he was seated again his full attention was refocused on the destruction of the White brothers.

*   *   *

Michael Pro had been assigned as Marla's cameraman for this evening's prayer meeting. He'd been thrilled about working with her, not only because her quality of work would help his career, but also because she was very cute. He wasn't thrilled about the assignment, however, since he was an atheist and as such, didn't believe in all this talk of miracles.

Michael had been scanning the large crowd and began focusing on Marla. She stood with head bowed and eyes closed as were most of the Christians in the tent. If he had believed in angels, she would have received his vote as being one. He scanned right and focused on Rev. Smith who was standing on the raised platform just in front of Michael. Michael's eyes grew wide in disbelief. He blinked and then blinked again.

He looked over at Marla Brinkle and said, "Pssst! Pssst!"

Marla looked up at Michael, who nodded toward the stage and as she turned to look all color drained from her stunned countenance. She tried to speak, but couldn't, at least not on her first attempt. She cleared her throat, faced the camera and forced herself to speak.

She whispered, "Rev. Smith, ladies and gentleman, please open your eyes and see the wonder that God has performed."

She turned toward the stage again and Michael followed her gaze with the camera. There was a collective gasp from the audience, as the closest people saw Joshua White and President Place fade into existence before their very eyes. A brilliant light that dazzled the audience surrounded them. Later, some reported they could see heavenly figures standing in that light, but before they could be sure the light was gone and the two confused humans stood alone before them. Joshua recovered first and shook Rev. Smith's extended hand, and then they embraced, joyful in this mighty reunion. Rev. Smith hugged President Place and the President hugged Joshua out of the sheer joy of their release.

Ellen ran up, "Joshua! Oh Joshua! Thank God you're safe!"

They hugged and kissed and laughed.

The audience laughed and hugged each other and all was joy and peace. Marla was tempted to run up there herself, but remembered her responsibility to her T.V. audience.

She, therefore, wiped the tears of joy from her face and said into the camera, "As you can see ladies and gentlemen, what started out to be a somber prayer meeting has turned into a celebration. For those of you who may have just tuned in, Joshua White and President Place have miraculously been returned to us out of thin air. We don't know how they got here or from where, but we'll soon find out. Let's just watch the joy for awhile, then we'll try to interview the President and Joshua."

Michael turned the camera back onto the stage and Marla Brinkle jumped up and down for joy.

*   *   *

Vice President Huggens was sitting in the President's desk chair in the Oval Office, with his feet propped up on the desk, laughing at the Christians on the television set.

He said, "When will they ever learn? They can't defeat us! Their friends are dead by now and I'll soon be President of the United States!"

He picked up the phone and pretended, "Tell the Prime Minister to wait, I'm busy!"

He pushed another button, "Send fifty-thousand troops to help...to help...Oh I don't care, to whoever needs them!"

Huggens put down the receiver and laughed. He was looking in drawers and pushing buttons when the knock came.

"Come in!", he exclaimed, jovially, without looking up.

A man in a business suit and three men in uniform walked in.

Huggens stood and asked, "What do you want here? The President isn't back yet!"

The man in the suit said, "Mr. Vice President, you haven't been watching your T.V. set have you? If you had, you'd know that just three minutes ago the President and Joshua White appeared on national television, seemingly out of thin air. On top of that, about ten minutes ago, we got a call from Hawk, one of our undercover agents, telling us that the President had been freed and that you were responsible for her abduction. The man pointed to the three uniformed officers and said, "These are Marine MP's, Mr. Vice President, and they're going to take you into custody until we can determine just what is going on around here."

Vice President Huggens tried to run, but he was no match for the three soldiers.

He shouted as they dragged him from the Oval Office, "But this was to be my office! You're ruining everything!"

The man in the suit turned off the light and closed the door as he whispered to himself, "We'll have the office fumigated in the morning."

*   *   *

There was a stir at the back of the crowd. Marla turned and ordered Michael to focus on the disturbance. Marla stood on her tiptoes and waved, her smile broadening as she saw Grady's red hair blazing at the back of the tent. He was steadily making his way toward Marla in the front. With him were three men in black suits and one man who looked like a gang member. He wore jeans, T-shirt and a bandanna around his head. He was tall and looked somewhat like Joshua White.

Marla forgot the camera and hugged Grady, kissed him and then said, "Did you see, Grady? Did you see what happened?"

Grady laughed and said, "I sure did! We were watching from my office and came straight over. It wasn't easy getting through the crowd, but I wanted Joshua to see his brother as soon as possible. Marla this is Jarrett White. Jarrett White this is my fiancée, Marla Brinkle."

They shook hands and Marla got a chill from the touch. She withdrew her hand nervously and looked into the man's eyes. They were cold and deep and horded a great deal of pain that can only be glimpsed through one's eyes. The feeling was gone as quickly as it had come and the group moved toward the stage.

Grady yelled, "Joshua! Hey Joshua, look who came to see you!"

Joshua turned and at first, he just stared as if in shock. Then he walked forward, a smile growing on his face as he came closer to the brother he hadn't seen or heard from in years.

Joshua embraced Jarrett and said, "Is it really you, Jarrett! After all this time? I'd given up hope!"

Jarrett hugged back, if not quite so enthusiastically, and said, "Yes, Josh it's me. It would appear that we have a lot to catch up on. Why don't we go off by ourselves and talk for awhile. I have a lot to tell you and a lot to ask you. OK?"

Joshua didn't hesitate. He told everyone that they were leaving and that he'd answer questions later. The crowd parted for them, as the Red Sea had for Moses and his people.

After they left, Director Aires approached the President and said, "Madam President. Hawk has informed me that your son and the doctor are safe and in our custody. Dr. Kamerman and Starvas Creen got away somehow, but we've begun a massive search for them. Finally, Vice President Huggens is in custody and is singing like a bird! It may take days to record all he has to say to us. Also, the man that left with Joshua White is Jarrett White known to you as Eagle."

The President gulped, "That's Eagle? One of our best under cover operatives?"

"Yes, Madam President. He started the Demon Slayer Gang. He collected fifty or so of the meanest, most wanted men in America and tonight he delivered them all into our hands. He has also kept in touch with Hawk, the woman who helped you tonight, and they have a lot of information about the Committee's activities. It should make for some interesting reading when they get their reports finished."

President Place said, "I'm sure of it, Aires. Well done! Now if you'll excuse me I have a press conference to give."

Aires looked nervous, "Excuse me Madam President, but this is all "Top Secret" information. Maybe we should brief you before you go live on television?"

The President smiled, "Too late for that Aires. You just gave your report to me on live television. I'd say that none of this information is classified any longer!"

Aires turned, then for the first time noticed the TV Camera and Marla Brinkle who held the microphone up close to them. His face turned red more angry at himself than at Marla. He turned back to the President and said, "I'll have my resignation to you by morning, good evening!"

"Oh nonsense, Aires! Stick around and enjoy the fruits of your labor."

With that she walked up to the microphone and told the world each and every detail of Dr. Kamerman's Committee. The abductions, the brainwashing and the blackmail of several Heads of State. Also, of his attempt to create the One World Order that he and men like him had orchestrated throughout history.

The President promised the nations of the world,

"I'll make it my personal business to make sure that your people are released from Dr. Kamerman's prison, given the proper psychiatric help to recover and returned to their duties, free of any outside interference. Thank you, citizens of the world."

It had taken the President some forty-five minutes to tell her story. During that time Marla had been in contact with her office. They were very pleased with her; their ratings were off the scale.

Marla ran up to the President **and** took the microphone from her but held her arm.

She said with a broad smile, "Madam President, I've just received word that your already high approval rating of 75 percent has just this minute topped out at an unheard of 98 percent! I believe that people are giving you their vote of confidence early, wouldn't you say?"

President Place smiled and said, "I want to thank the citizens of the United States for that, but please remember to go out and actually cast your vote next month when it counts. *Thank you.*"

Marla filled the space just vacated by the President, and said, "This has been a live report from Jesus Park in the City of Covenant. To recap..."

CHAPTER TWENTY-ONE

REUNION

Joshua White had given his brother, Jarrett, a tour of Jesus Park and had shown him all the different plans that he had put into effect.

"And this will be our new chapel."

Jarrett's mind was obviously on other things.

Joshua smiled, "All right Jarrett, the tour's over. Thanks for enduring it. Why don't you tell me what's really on your mind?"

Jarrett stared at Joshua for a minute and then said, "I never could fool you, could I?"

"Nope! So what's up?"

Jarrett took a deep breath and spat out the next sentence with tears forming in his eyes, "Brother Keller raped me when I was fourteen! There I've said it!"

He began to cry.

Joshua put his hand on Jarrett's shoulder and said, "I'm so sorry. I had no idea. When? Where?"

Through sobs that he hadn't allowed himself over the years Jarrett spilled the entire woeful story:

He wept, "It was just after my fourteenth birthday. I'd helped him with Vacation Bible School and we were cleaning up. He started rubbing against me and touching me. I was shocked and thought that it must be a mistake! I moved away and worked at cleaning the next table. Without warning I was hit on the head from behind and I must have been knocked-out for a moment. When I came to he'd pulled my pants off and he was..." Jarrett couldn't finish.

He broke into a shameless bout of cleansing weeping that began the healing process.

Joshua held him tightly and said, "Shush now, it's all right. You'll be all right now."

Sadness for his brother and anger at Brother Keller was about to break his heart. Joshua had always thought that Brother Keller was the best elder his church had ever had. He'd always been so good with the kids, or so it had been thought.

Joshua gently prodded, "Was that the only time?"

Jarrett, through gasps of weeping said, "Afterwards, he told me if I told anyone he'd kill our parents! He had his way with me many times by using that threat. I loved our parents and didn't want them hurt, but I couldn't take it anymore either. So one day I snapped. As you know, it was shortly after my sixteenth birthday. Keller had just used me again and I was so ashamed! I thought of killing myself but, for some reason, that didn't seem to be the answer. I climbed on that new motorcycle that mom and dad had given me for my birthday and just rode off.

There were many times I wanted to tell you guys, but I just couldn't! I wrote that short note saying that I had to go find my own way in life and I just left. As the years went by I wanted to call or write, but I didn't know what to say. I knew there'd be questions and I didn't have the answers!"

During the conversation, Joshua had been leading Jarrett toward his car.

When they got there Joshua said, "Let's take a ride, shall we?"

Jarrett agreed and got in.

He continued his story, "I wandered around aimlessly for a couple of years and, at eighteen, I joined the army. I did very well in the army because the hidden anger that was growing into rage drove me hard and I excelled in everything. Before long, I was approached to join the Special Forces. I excelled in that as well; and when it was time for me to get out, I had a decision to make. I could re-enlist or I could join the CIA as an undercover agent. At this point, I was well into dangerous adventure, so I joined the latter and here I am!"

Jarrett revealed to Joshua some of the adventures he'd had over the years, ending with this last assignment of gathering the most wanted men in America.

"I picked the name of my gang, **'The Demon Slayers'** because of you, Joshua. I'd seen what you'd done here in Covenant for the Lord over the years and I thought as a joke I'd encode my name. Since I was gathering what most people would call demons and I was in fact going to turn them in, I was a demon slayer."

Joshua smiled and said, "You're closer to the mark than you could've ever imagined, Jarrett. These men are possessed by actual demons as you yourself were until you came here. You're being protected for a time so that you can bring a new direction to your life. And we're about to begin that new direction!"

Jarrett looked shocked at this talk of demons and protection thinking back to his experience in Sister Gen's trailer.

Jarrett was about to ask a question when Joshua said, "We've arrived."

Jarrett looked out the window of the car, "Here? At a nursing home?"

Joshua got out and said, "Come on you'll see what I mean."

They walked down the hall in silence and came to room 222. They went in and stood next to a bed holding a very old, very paralyzed man.

Joshua said, "Brother Keller I brought someone to see you. It's my brother, Jarrett White."

Brother Keller's eyes opened wide with terror and fear. Jarrett's eyes reflected fear and hate, as he stared down at the man who'd caused him so much pain over the years of his life.

Joshua said, "Brother Keller had a stroke shortly after you left. He's been in this condition all these years. He needs your forgiveness, Jarrett, as much as you need to give it. Until you do, this will haunt you all of your life. Remember the Lord Jesus first forgave you all of your sins."

Jarrett pulled away from Joshua's grasp and said, "I'll see him in hell before I'll forgive him!"

With that Jarrett turned and hastily exited the room.

When Joshua came outside he found Jarrett leaning against a tree sobbing softly.

Jarrett whispered, "How could you do that to me Joshua?"

He sounded so betrayed that it broke Joshua's heart, "I wanted you to face Brother Keller and forgive him. It's the only way to put this behind you. Look,

Jarrett, the Lord's Kingdom is made of love and forgiveness. There's no room for hate and long term grudges. It only eats away at your own soul and festers there, keeping you from the relationship with Jesus that you deserve. Please try to see what I'm saying, Jarrett. By forgiving Brother Keller you can be free of this horrible experience once and for all!"

Jarrett said, "I just don't know if I can, Josh. I've hated that pathetic creature for so long it's almost a habit."

Josh said, "That's how it is with sin and hatred. It becomes habitual and we get comfortable with it. It lives in our hearts making them harder and harder, until we can no longer love or forgive the way we were commanded to by our Lord Jesus."

Jarrett spoke his own arguments, but as Josh listened something caught his eye. At first, he didn't know what it was. It was dark, but they could see each other in the light of the mercury-vapor street lamp on the corner. Josh concentrated on Jarrett's face and when he saw the red dot move slightly on Jarrett's forehead, he knew what it was.

"A laser targeting sight!", Josh thought as he screamed, "Noooo!"

Josh knew the probable consequences of his action as he jumped forward embracing Jarrett in one last life saving embrace. He wouldn't let his brother die until he'd accepted the Lord Jesus, no matter what the cost.

Jarrett, who was spilling his heart out to his brother, barely noticed Josh's change of expression. An instant after Josh jumped toward him to embrace him, Jarrett watched Josh's neck and upper chest explode and then Jarrett's own face exploded with a searing pain, which was the last conscious sensation that Jarrett White experienced.

*   *   *

Aaron was sad that his duty of guarding Joshua White had come to an end.

As Josh came out of his lifeless body and stood once again next to Aaron he said, "I have so much to do yet, Aaron! Are you sure it's my time?"

Aaron smiled and said, "We don't make mistakes, Josh. You've done many wonderful things in your life, things to be proud of, but it's to be left to others now."

Josh thought sadly, "But what of Ellen, she'll be devastated to lose yet another man she loved. We had so many plans."

Aaron countered, "Yes, as well you should have; however, she'll be fine. The Lord has many wonderful things in store for Ellen White just as he has for Jarrett."

Josh looked down and saw his own lifeless body lying on top of his brother. He'd jumped pretty high and his neck and chest had covered Jarrett's head. The bullet had crashed into Josh and then through him, knocking both he and Jarrett to the ground. Jarrett was covered in blood, most of it Josh's, but he was still breathing.

Josh heard a laugh and looked further down the street. There he saw Dr. Kamerman and Starvas Creen getting into their car.

Starvas was saying, "Can you believe it, both in one shot! This is a record! Well doctor, you don't have to worry about them any longer!"

Josh shook his head and said, "Aaron, if only these people could see the ugly demons they support!"

They watched as the doctor and Creen drove away with the sneering Captain Rumpus and Lt. Crygen in tow.

Aaron looked back at Josh and said, "It's time to go Josh. Don't worry! The Lord's in control and He has plans that will take care of things down here. He also has work lined up for you in Heaven. You'll be as valuable there as you ever were here. Are you ready?"

Josh took one last look at Jarrett, "Can't we get him help first?"

Aaron laughed, "Caring about others more than yourself is a hard habit for you to break isn't it?"

Without waiting for an answer Aaron waved his hand causing the front door of the nursing home to rattle loudly bringing a nurse to investigate. When she saw the bodies, she screamed and ran back inside to call an ambulance.

Aaron said, "Now can we go?"

Josh smiled sheepishly and nodded.

Aaron touched Josh's shoulder and they disappeared in a flash of radiant pure white light.

Josh hugged Patty, then his mom and dad, and finally he hugged Jesus, Himself.

Jesus told Joshua, "Well done my good and faithful servant. Welcome home!"

The group walked the streets of the Heavenly City and stopped before a large mansion on a hill. It looked like the same magnificent mansion that Joshua had visited before. The one in which his parents lived.

Patty saw his confused expression and said, "Yes,

Josh it's the same mansion but with an additional wing for us."

She said that last with a broad smile on her face and Josh responded with a warm smile of his own. They hugged and Joshua knew he was finally home. He knew he'd finally found wholeness and purpose.

Jesus said, "All right everyone, it's time for Josh to meet with our Father face to face. You're to see Him as he actually is!"

Josh stepped away from Patty, his excitement growing. Jesus put his arm around Josh and they faded together into the presence of God the Father and Josh was forever changed.

CHAPTER TWENTY-TWO

SACRIFICE

It was suddenly hot; Jarrett brushed his sweaty forehead with his right hand and almost hit himself with the hammer he was holding. In his left he held a large spike, the purpose of which he couldn't fathom.

He became aware of the crowd around him. They were cheering and shouting indiscernible expletives and Jarrett was very disoriented. Suddenly a man dressed in a strange uniform yelled at him to get busy. He looked to his right and saw a man, kneeling as Jarrett was, and he too had a hammer in one hand and a spike in the other.

It was only then that Jarrett noticed the man lying on the wooden cross beneath him. Suddenly, it seemed the most natural thing in the world to him. He took his spike, placed it against the man's hand and pounded it home with his hammer.

He felt the spike pierce the flesh, muscle and tendons of the hand. He heard the bones crack as the spike passed through them and finally sink itself into the wood beyond. He continued to pound until the head of the spike was even with the flesh. He then stood up and helped secure the ropes which were used to raise the cross bar that bore the man up to the hook where the cross bar was to be secured.

Jarrett stood below the cross and surveyed his work with pride. He seemed to remember doing this many times to different people, but this man was different somehow! Jarrett was just wondering who this man was when one of the state employed workers put a ladder up against his cross. He climbed it and nailed a plaque above the man's head.

Jarrett read, "Jesus of Nazareth. King of the Jews!"

Jarrett laughed and yelled, "A king? Doesn't look like a king to me!"

Jesus looked down at Jarrett with his calm warm loving eyes, and said, "Jarrett White! This sacrifice is for you! You are forgiven! Now go! Love and forgive others as I have forgiven you!"

The wind, which had begun to pick up now, howled between the three crosses. The sky turned dark and the ground began to shake. The scene had quickly turned nightmarish and the crowd began to run and scream about the doom they felt was imminent.

Jarrett stood his ground, defiantly glaring at this Jesus.

He yelled, "I will not forgive Keller! Do you hear me Jesus? I will not!"

The blood that had been flowing freely from the body of this man named Jesus had begun to slow. A guard walked up and pierced the man's side with his spear. The little blood and water that was left in the man's body was carried by the wind and splashed directly into Jarrett's face. It burned like acid and he fell to the ground screaming in pain. It was only in Jesus' death that Jarrett White realized that God Himself had just touched him.

Jarrett climbed to his knees and cried out, "What have I done? I've killed my Lord and Savior! The same one that Josh serves so faithfully!"

Through his pain and blurred vision, Jarrett, suddenly saw Josh kneeling next to him.

Josh whispered, "We've all taken part in the Lord's crucifixion through our sins, Jarrett, but he has forgiven you as he forgives all that accept Him as their Savior!

"Jarrett, please come, serve the Lord and enjoy life to the fullest. Believe me it's great here in Heaven!"

Josh began to disappear and Jarrett grabbed for him, but he missed. Leaping to his feet he shouted, "Please don't go, Josh."

Jarrett heard a female voice, "Now calm down, Mr. White! It's all right; you're in the hospital. You've been through quite an ordeal."

The nurse turned to an aide and said, "Go get Dr. Hammerstein and call Rev. Smith. Tell them the patient is finally awake!"

*   *   *

Rev. Smith sat next to Ellen. They were in the large chapel tent in Jesus Park sitting in the front row as they had everyday for the last four days. The line of people, which flowed past Joshua, was endless. People had flown in from around the world to visit Joshua White one last time. Crippled people had touched his dead body and had been healed!

Ellen had said, "Even in death, the Lord honors Josh's service to God."

Ellen was exhausted, hurt and filled with more grief than she'd ever thought possible. People had been very supportive of course, but only time would mend her broken heart!

She turned to Rev. Smith, "I'll miss him so much, Jonathon!"

He nodded, "We all will, Ellen, we all will!"

Rev. Smith looked up as one of the ushers approached and said, "Pastor, Jarrett White is awake. They're asking for you to come over."

He looked at Ellen and asked, "Do you mind if I go over there for awhile Ellen?"

She bravely replied, "No, of course not. I'll be fine. You must explain things to Josh's brother. Josh loved Jarrett so much! I'm glad that he got to see him one last time before he..."

Rev. Smith gave her a hug, got up and left leaving Fr. Powell to sit with Ellen.

*   *   *

Worl and Aaron flew high above Jesus Park and were pleased at the response the people of the world were showing toward Josh's life.

As they flew back to their troops, Aaron stated, "The Lord's work will now spread faster than ever. The enemy always fails to realize that the more they try to stamp out the Spirit of the Lord, the more they actually spread His influence over the world!"

Worl smiled, "And just think Aaron, the adventure isn't over yet! The greatest wonders of the Lord still lie ahead of us! Have you given Andy his final instructions concerning Jarrett White's conversion?"

Aaron nodded, "Yes, he's been praying and interceding for him since the incident. He feels that

Jarrett's heart will melt, after a time. All attempts by the enemy to reach Jarrett have failed."

Worl, satisfied that everything was moving according to plan, took his leave of Aaron and headed for his next assignment.

War was a never-ending transfer from one battle to another. Aaron remained at his post over Covenant to be sure things proceeded in the proper order and at the proper speed.

At Aaron's signal, a legion of angels joined him in praising and honoring the "Name of the Most High God, the Lord Jesus Christ".

CHAPTER TWENTY-THREE
FAREWELL TO A FRIEND

Capt. Rumpus stood as the messenger hurried in.

"Report! Come on give! What news from Covenant?"

The messenger was out of breath as he fell to his knees before, Rumpus, his new lord.

He said through bated breath, "Master, I bear bad tidings, I'm afraid. We've done everything we can to get to the human, Jarrett White, but the angel forces are mighty in that region. We lost over five thousand demons in our last push alone and I suppose we've lost even more by now. The inner guard cuts down what few demons make it through the outer perimeter of angels. They'll not let us get within two miles of the man."

Rumpus had listened to the message with no visible reaction. He stood motionless for several minutes, then looked at the messenger, "Call off all troops! There's no use losing anymore to this! We'll leave Jarrett White to the enemy, for now at least. Who cares? We're patient. We'll wait until the right opportunity presents itself and then make our move."

He looked over at Lt. Crygen commanding, "Lt. Crygen! Assign an observer for me. Someone who's both patient and dependable. He's to watch Jarrett White from the moment he can get close enough until the moment there's something that we can use. Those assigned are to report back to me personally, is that understood?"

Lt. Crygen, who still didn't like working for Rumpus and unable to do anything about it, said, "Yes sir! I'll get right on it, sir!"

As Lt. Crygen left, Capt. Rumpus turned to the messenger and shouted, "What are you waiting for? Get on your way and sound the retreat!"

The messenger, who'd been hoping for a meal and some rest, left unsatisfied.

Capt. Rumpus sat back on his new throne and passed the time by condemning some of Tumult's faithful troops to death. His new power was immense and he was enjoying the freedom to wield it as he saw fit. He was also basking in the knowledge that when the time was right, he would totally destroy Jarrett White!

*   *   *

Jarrett found himself standing in the desert with sweat dripping down his forehead into his eyes. He turned in circles but all he could see for miles around was sand. Then something caught his eye; a distorted shape moved toward him. Whatever it was disturbed the sand as it came closer, throwing it high into the air. Try as he might he could not make out what it was. The heat rising up from the desert floor rippled the distance with distortions and fear began to grip his heart.

Questions raced through his thoughts, *Where am I? Why am I here? Who or what is that shape racing toward me?'*

Then it came back to him; someone had tried to kill him. He whispered, "Joshua.", as the memory returned of Joshua leaving him alone. Jarrett had called out to

Joshua not to go but he had left him anyway. Jarrett fell to the ground and in both frustration and anger he began to pound the sand with his fists. He remembered the kind gentle eyes of the man he had crucified via his own sins. He also remembered the love and forgiveness that the man freely shared with him. Jarrett fell forward, buried his head in his arms and wept.

Just then a distant roar reached his ears and he sat up, wiped his eyes with the part of his sleeve that was not covered in sand, and held a hand over his eyes to cut the sun's glare. The shape was much closer now and Jarrett thought he recognized both the sound and the sight of the shape. Yes, he was sure of it now - it was his white motorcycle. Someone had come to rescue him.

He was still sitting in the sand when the motorcycle slid to a stop, showering Jarrett with sand. When the deluge cleared he saw not only his white motorcycle but also its two occupants.

Joshua was riding behind the large angel, Worl, and as Josh got off, Jarrett jumped up, ran to him and they embraced.

Jarrett stated, plaintively, "I thought you had left me for good Josh."

Josh patted his back and said, "We are eternal beings Jarrett, and there is no such thing as leaving each other forever. I must leave for a time but we will be together soon enough."

Worl had gotten off of the cycle during this exchange and he now spoke to Jarrett, "Jarrett I have news from our Lord and your Savior, Jesus Christ. He apologizes for having to advance you so quickly but he will be needing you sooner than you would normally be ready. Just remember that our God is all powerful and He will fill you with the power and wisdom that you need when you need it."

Jarrett had no idea what Worl was talking about and told him so.

Worl smiled and said, "It is not important that you understand just yet Jarrett, but when God begins to work His plans through you, just remember my message and cooperate."

Joshua hugged his brother again and said, I'll be praying for you brother. You must carry on where I left off."

With that Joshua and Worl remounted the motorcycle, with Joshua driving this time. As Josh started the engine Worl reached around him and tore off one of the side mirrors of the motorcycle and handed it to Jarrett. As Jarrett took the mirror he felt an electrical type charge enter his body and heard Worl as his voice easily boomed clearly over the engine noise, "This mirror will be a sign to you that this was no dream. Believe us and obey Jesus."

They both waved as the motorcycle sped away from Jarrett. Jarrett looked at their receding shape, then down at the mirror that he held in his hands as he thought, *What just happened here. Why do I feel, what? Power? Filling every cell in my body?'*

Before he could seek for answers to his questions the desert floor began to move in a whirlpool motion. Jarret panicked as he sank quickly below the surface of the sandy desert floor.

*   *   *

He had been digging for what seemed an eternity. Scratching really. Scratching his way upward, always upward toward the light. When he finally broke the surface he took one long shuddering breath.

Jarrett White tried to speak but only a raspy croak came out of his mouth. He thrashed in panic just as Dr. Hammerstein walked through the door of Jarrett's hospital room.

The doctor moved quickly to Jarrett's bed, speaking reassuringly, "Mr. White calm down, please, and don't try to talk. You can't speak because your jaw is wired shut and the tissue of your throat is swollen. I spoke to Director Aires about you and he told me to shoot straight with you. Is that the way you'd like it? Just nod your head once if you agree."

Jarrett nodded his head once and waited to hear more. The doctor pulled a chair up to the bed, sat down and continued, "Your brother Joshua White is dead. The bullet passed through his spine and came out his chest. As it made its exit, the bullet went through your right cheek and embedded itself deep into your jawbone, shattering the bone in several places. The bullet also damaged a lot of your jaw muscles and tissues. I had to do a lot of reconstructive surgery to put it all back in place. You still face several surgeries in which I'll eventually replace all of the damaged tissue. When I'm finished you'll look normal, but you'll not look the same. Aires said that in your profession, especially after this last assignment, having a different face could be a plus. You'll be uncomfortable for awhile, but you don't have any life threatening wounds."

Jarrett tried to speak with the same results.

"Please, Mr. White, don't try to talk, you'll rip something loose! Here try to write down what you want to say."

The doctor handed him a pad of paper and a pencil.

Jarrett wrote, "How long have I been out?"

"You've been out for about four days now."

He wrote, "Is my brother buried already?"

The doctor smiled, "Oh no, Mr. White! There have been people coming to see him from all over the world! He's lying in state at Jesus Park and the President of the United States has provided him with her own Marine Guard. He'll be buried with full military, police and Presidential honors! Flowers line the streets of Jesus Park leading to the main meeting tent, ending in a literal forest of floral colors and scents. It's actually quite beautiful, Mr. White. On top of that, the line of visitors hasn't let up for the entire four-day period you've been unconscious. People are staying at the park all night, in order to be in place for tomorrow's funeral service. Your brother was a great man, Mr. White, and people are honoring his memory and sacrifice."

Jarrett wrote, "I have to be there for his service. You take me in this bed if you have to, but get me there!"

At that moment, Rev. Smith entered the room and quickly apologized, "Oh, I'm sorry, doctor; I didn't realize you were here, I'll just..."

The doctor said, "That's all right, Pastor, we're just discussing Mr. White's trip to the funeral tomorrow."

The pastor looked surprised but pleased, "Will he be able to attend doctor?"

"I think it'll be all right as long as he goes in a

wheel chair and *stays in it*! Do you understand, Mr. White? No trying to walk on your own!"

Jarrett wrote, "I'll be good."

The doctor smiled and said, "Oh, I almost forgot Mr. White. The police wanted me to inform you that your motorcycle has been stolen. I'm sorry."

Thoughts of the desert, sand, and a single motorcycle mirror raced through Jarrett's thoughts. Then he wrote, "Did they find anything?"

The doctor thought and then said, "I didn't think much of it at the time but now that you ask, they did say that they found only one of your side mirrors lying on the ground where your bike had been. They figure it got torn off during their escape with the bike."

The corners of Jarrett's mouth turned up slightly as he thought, *'It wasn't a dream.'*

Then he wrote, "Rev. Smith could you take me to see Brother Keller at the nursing home?"

"I suppose I can take you to see him, Mr. White, but he's not at the nursing home any longer. It seems that shortly after you and Joshua visited him the other night, he had another stroke. They don't expect him to live very long at all."

Jarrett wrote, "Please call me Jarrett! I want to see Brother Keller right now! I owe it to Josh to see the man before he dies."

The doctor and the pastor looked at each other, shrugged their shoulders and the doctor went to get a wheelchair. They both helped Jarrett out of bed and into his new means of transportation.

Jarrett pointed to the pad of paper and pencil, but the doctor laughed and said, "I'm afraid, Jarrett, that Mr.

Keller can't read in his condition. I doubt that he'll even notice that we're there."

Jarrett insisted, however, and when it was handed to him he wrote, "Pastor, I want you to read whatever I write. Read it to Brother Keller whether he can hear it or not! OK?"

"All right, Jarrett, no problem."

The doctor tagged along more out of curiosity than anything else. He wanted to keep an eye on Jarrett's progress, as he left his bed, so he could decide if Jarrett actually was strong enough to attend the funeral.

When Rev. Smith pushed Jarrett up to Keller's bed, Jarrett wrote, "Brother Keller please listen to me! I forgive you for what you did to me all those years ago. You've suffered enough. I seriously hope this God, that Josh loved so much, can hear this and that he'll forgive you all of your sins, whether they were done to me or some other innocent child. I don't know what's moving me to do this. I've hated you so much for too long. Recently, however, I've learned that Jesus died for my sins and now my own brother has died to save my wretched life. I owe it to Josh to make something of myself and to serve this Jesus whom I still don't know very well. Please forgive me my hatred against you Brother Keller!"

Jarrett had written, frantically, and hoped that Rev. Smith could read it. Rev. Smith read it to Brother Keller, who showed no sign that he'd heard a single word.

Jarrett wrote, "Please read it again, louder this time!"

This time as Rev. Smith read the message Jarrett reached out and shook Keller's arm. When Keller opened his eyes Rev. Smith started over and read even louder.

After the pastor was finished, Brother Keller smiled with that part of his face that still worked and reached out a shaking hand toward Jarrett. Jarrett took the man's hand and he watched as death dulled Keller's eyes.

Brother Keller came out of his cloudy existence and heard Rev. Smith's voice. He couldn't believe the message that he was hearing. He'd longed to ask for forgiveness but couldn't, so he'd prayed for it instead. Now on his last day on earth, Jarrett White gave that forgiveness!

"The Lord does indeed work in mysterious ways", was the last thought that Brother Keller had on this side of Heaven.

Keller watched as the angel bent down, took his hand and pulled him from his lifeless body. The joy that had filled his heart at Jarrett's touch was overshadowed by the touch of this heavenly being.

Without a word, but with much love and care, the angel wrapped the new saint in his protective wings and soared toward his heavenly home.

Rev. Smith and Dr. Hammerstein both stood wiping tears from their eyes as they watched Jarrett holding Brother Keller's lifeless hand. They'd never witnessed such human love and forgiveness. Neither knew why Jarrett was forgiving Keller, but neither did they miss the struggle that took place to give that forgiveness.

Rev. Smith said, "Jarrett, I know that Joshua would've been very proud of you this night."

The three men prayed together. They had

witnessed the death of one person and the rebirth of another.

*   *   *

The crowd of over one hundred thousand Christian friends sitting or standing in complete silence at Joshua's gravesite, as well as, millions watching on television listened to the haunting sounds of the bagpipe. Grady moving slowly and mournfully, but ever onward toward Josh's casket, allowed his music to grow louder stirring the hearts of all who heard. When he reached the casket of his friend, he abruptly ceased playing his woeful dirge. Grady was dressed in his full Irish Kilt Uniform and looked as impressive as his pipes sounded. He saluted in a slow exaggerated salute of honor and was simultaneously joined by the over five thousand military and police personnel present. When their hands again reached their sides, Grady pumped air into the bagpipes and continued his playing as he marched away. At about ten steps from the casket, he was joined first by two more pipers, then ten, then twenty. There were over a hundred pipers, in all, giving a very impressive and moving tribute. As the last of the mournful notes had escaped from their pipes and were mere echoes, there wasn't a dry eye in the cemetery. This was followed by the Marine Band as well as several other military and police bands who, displayed their own skills in honoring their fallen comrade. They played a mixture of patriotic and Christian music that swelled the hearts of the audience and brought new tears to the already red and swollen eyes of the participants.

Jarrett sat with Ellen on one side of him and Marla on the other. The President and Pastor Smith stood by the casket. When the fanfare was over and all was quiet once again, Ellen got up and hugged Jarrett and Marla. As she walked up to the microphone, the police and the military, as if one large body, snapped to attention causing some to jump in startled surprise. Ellen gave Pastor Smith and President Place a hug as she passed them.

There was a squeal from the speakers as Ellen opened her Bible to Galatians 5:22 and 23, and read, "But the fruit of the Spirit is love, joy, peace, longsuffering, gentleness, goodness, faith, meekness, temperance: against such there is no law."

She closed the Bible, looked out at the crowd and said, "My fiancée, Joshua White, was all of these things and more." Thunderous applause arose from the crowd.

Ellen continued, "He served us well and he had many adventures. I keep hoping that the Lord may yet raise him up from this casket, but I don't think He will, not this time."

Ellen looked at the casket and her voice broke as she said, "I love you, Josh!"

She began to cry and said, "I'm sorry! I thought I could do this but I just can't continue."

Rev. Smith helped Ellen back to her seat as President Place took her position at the microphone, "Joshua White was a good friend to me. He helped my son be cured of a terminal illness. He brought me to my senses so that I could lead this country in the light of God's word and he helped to save my eternal soul by leading me back to the Lord Jesus. Joshua, how will I, or any of the other thousands of people that you've helped, ever thank you?" President Place stepped back too choked to continue.

Jarrett White rolled his wheelchair up to Rev. Smith and handed him a paper which instructed him to read the following, "Jarrett White, Josh's brother, has requested that I read from Luke 9:24. It reads, 'For whosoever will save his life shall lose it: but whosoever will lose his life for my sake, the same shall save it.' Jarrett adds, 'I will endeavor to live up to my brother's example and his sacrifice.'"

As Jarrett rolled his chair blindly backward, he accidentally ran into a young woman named Melanie who'd been blind since birth. She felt the chair hit her legs and grunted as she fell forward catching herself on Jarrett's muscular shoulders. As soon as her hands touched his shoulders, she had to cover her eyes to protect them from the glare of the sun. Her eyes began to water first from their sudden ability to see and then from the sheer joy that Melanie now felt. She yelled to no one in particular, "I can see! I can see! I touched someone and now I can see."

Ellen rushed to Melanie's side and wiped the girl's eyes with her handkerchief. Melanie opened her eyes, she blinked and squinted against the brightness of the sun that she'd never seen. She looked down and saw the shock in the eyes of the man sitting in the wheel chair, his face and head encased in bandages.

She praised him saying, "You've given me my sight, Mr. White! You've received your brother's gift of healing! I want to thank you from the bottom of my heart. She bent over and kissed his forehead, her tears mixing with his.

The funeral of Joshua White was forgotten as word of the miracle spread throughout the crowd and what followed was unsolicited, joyous and perhaps even glorious pandemonium! The crowd surged toward Jarrett, everyone trying to touch him at once. He could quite literally feel the crush of humanity on his shoulders.

Secret Service agents moved in to surround Jarrett and the President, quickly escorting them toward the waiting helicopter where the pilot was already starting its engines to expedite a swift and timely retreat.

As they flew over the vast crowd filling Jesus Park to over-flowing, Jarrett White said a silent farewell to his brother Joshua. A brother whom he would dearly love to question right about now!

He thought, "*What just happened? How did I generate the power that I felt go through me when the girl was healed? I didn't ask for this nor do I deserve it, but I know that Worl and my brother had a hand in it.*' It was a calming thought and he decided to obey God's call regardless of his opinion on the subject.

President Place was watching him closely and even though the bandages hid his expression she could see the questions in his eyes.

She said, "It would appear Jarrett that Joshua not only gave you his life, but apparently gave you part of his soul as well." Jarrett wrote on his pad and handed it to the President. It read, "Joshua always did have a sense of humor!"

They laughed together, free for perhaps the first

time in their lives; they both understood the passage of Scripture found in I Corinthians 8:11.

The President quoted it in a whisper as Jarrett looked toward an uncertain future, "And through thy knowledge shall the weak brother perish, for whom Christ died?"

Joshua and his angels had made sure that Jarrett didn't perish in his sins.

Jarrett thought, *"Can I do any less for those I may come to know as brother?"*

CHAPTER TWENTY-FOUR
NEW BEGINNINGS

Satan sat on his huge ebony throne, his elbows resting on its arms, the fingertips of both of his hands gently tapping his lips as he glared down at the cowering Tumult. Sweat was pouring from Tumult's newly attached head as he awaited his final fate. He dreaded the horrors that he knew he must endure due to the utter failure of his mission.

Satan stood and the multitude of demons that'd been holding their collective breaths gasped as they saw his expression darken even more. He descended slowly at first but quickened his pace as he drew closer to Tumult. When he reached him, Satan backhanded him first on one cheek then on the other.

His voice dripped dangerously with anger as he whispered, "I trusted you to win this battle, Tumult! I gave you a second chance against my better judgment and now you've handed me another utter defeat!"

With a movement swifter than the demons could follow, Satan reached over drew Tumult's sword, swung it in a circle over his head and swished it toward Tumult's exposed throat. All demons present sat forward and licked their lips in anticipation of Tumult's demise. The blade stopped just short of Tumult's throat, however.

The demons moaned with disappointment.

Satan snarled, "No! That would be too easy for you! You must suffer greatly for this crime against me!"

Pacing back and forth while biting one of his long

nails, Satan studied Tumult. An evil smile appeared on his face and then with swift, slicing movements Satan removed Tumult's legs and hands.

Tumult glared up at Satan through his fear, hatred and pain threatening, "You better destroy me totally, Satan, or one of these days I'll kill you and take your place!"

"Nice try Tumult, but like I said that would be too easy. No! You'll be sent to the tar pits with the human souls, many of who have you to thank for their eternal punishment. They will be allowed to torment and torture you for a millennia or so, then what's left of you will crawl around in the filth of the torture dungeon, cleaning up after my personal entertainment. Yes, that's my command!"

The demons present sighed their approval, "Aaah!"

As Satan ascended to his throne, he yelled, "Away with this traitor!"

One demon guard picked up Tumult's legs and hands while three others grabbed the struggling but pathetic, former general's torso.

As he was carried away, Tumult shouted, "I'll get you for this Satan! If it's the last thing I do, I'll get you for this!"

Satan laughed and said, "Give it your best shot, loser!"

He turned with a flourish, his robes rustling as they whipped around behind him, and moved to his throne of power.

Satan called to the guards, "Bring in Rumpus!"

Rumpus, now mighty general, looked magnificent in his highly polished armor complete with flowing purple cape which dragged the floor behind him as he walked up the stairs toward his lord Satan. When he arrived at Satan's feet, Rumpus knelt on his right knee and kissed Satan's feet.

Satan reached down and tapped Rumpus' shoulders, a sign that he could rise. When Rumpus had risen, he stood with his head bowed in respect to his master.

Satan stood and said loudly so that all present could hear, "My fellow demons, this is Rumpus my new General Extreme! His power is only second to my own, is that understood?"

All present roared, "Hail the mighty Rumpus! May his mission be fulfilled!"

Satan allowed the shouts of joy and encouragement for a time and then raised his hand for silence that was instantaneous. He held up Tumult's bent and sorry excuse of a sword and as he held it, fire jumped from his fingertips to the sword. The glare was so incandescent that most had to turn away to protect their eyes. Not Rumpus, however, he wanted to see this transformation with his own eyes! As he watched, he saw the hilt of the sword glow bright with new jewels and he especially enjoyed the "Jewel of Power" that reappeared on the end of the hilt. The double-edged blade glowed with new strength and radiance, and even grew a couple of inches longer than Tumult's original sword!

When the transformation was complete and the glow had subsided, Satan handed Rumpus his new sword and spoke, "Rumpus, serve me bravely, serve me well, and together we will fill this Hell with the puny souls of Earth's humans!"

Cheers echoed off of the walls of the chamber as Satan led his new general into the banquet hall.

When all present were seated and ready to eat, Rumpus stood with goblet in hand and said, "Lord. Fellow demons. Tonight we celebrate!"

There were roars of agreement all around and Satan even smiled.

Rumpus continued, "Tomorrow, however, we'll launch plans for the most daring and bold attack to date! In this next battle, we'll draw even Christians into our deception and we'll finally bring them to their knees! Their leader, Joshua White, is gone thanks to my cunning and, of course my Lord's leadership. They have no one to replace him! Our victory is assured!"

Pandemonium broke out as their premature victory celebration continued all through the night.

* * *

President Place stood as they brought in the shackled Vice President Huggens. She rounded her desk and met them in the center of the room. Before anyone could react, Roberta, unexpectedly slapped Huggens across his right cheek. His head jerked to the side.

As her handprint turned red on his cheek, she said, "That's for endangering my son."

Again she slapped him, but this time a backhand on his left cheek, "That's for endangering everyone else!"

President Place immediately felt guilty for her less than Christian behavior, so she resisted the urge to strike him again. She squared her shoulders, straightened her jacket and went back around her desk.

As she sat down, she said, "I'm sorry for hitting you, Philip. I really hope you'll forgive me." Without waiting for an answer she continued, "All right, Phillip, here's the deal. You make a full and complete confession about your entire involvement giving us details of the Committee's operation and we'll see to it that you have a secure private cell for the rest of your life. Otherwise, we'll just put you in with the general population at our nearest maximum security prison and you can take your chances. Agreed?"

Huggens just nodded his head, but kept looking at the floor in shame. He was a crushed and empty man. Not even his own Spirit Guide had stayed to help him; the demons no longer needed him.

President Place said in disgust, "Take this traitor from my sight!"

They dragged him from the room as Director Aires said, "Are you ready for your next visitors, Madam President?"

Roberta smiled, "Yes, by all means send them in."

Again she stood. This time, however, she had a smile on her face. She rounded her desk and waited as Hawk and Eagle were led into the Oval Office. She barely recognized the pair. Hawk was wearing a very stylish suit. Her hair was styled and her makeup was perfect. She was quite beautiful. Eagle, too, had been transformed. He still had a half facial cast on and would for another month, but his hair was cut shorter and styled. His earrings were gone and his happy eyes spoke of a lighter soul than when they'd first met. The pair stood at attention awaiting orders.

Roberta smiled and said, "First, let me thank you

for the sacrifices you've both made for your country and our God. You've done a wonderful job and as a reward I'm awarding you both the Congressional Medal Of Honor!"

With that she turned took the medals from the top of her desk and hung them on the chests of Hawk and Eagle.

She then said, "I'm sorry that I can't give them publicly, but you don't exist, officially speaking, and it might actually endanger you.

"As a further reward, I'm offering you each a year off with pay so you can rest and recuperate. What do you say?"

Both Eagle and Hawk nodded and said, "Thank you, Madam President."

"At the end of that time, you'll be reactivated and given new assignments, either together or separately, depending upon the assignment.

"What'll you do with yourselves in between check-ins with Director Aires here?"

Eagle spoke first, "I'll spend my year at Jesus Park in Covenant learning more about this Jesus to whom I'm thinking of dedicating my life and I'll try to learn to accept and then use this new power of healing that I seem to have."

He turned to Hawk and asked, "Why don't you come with me, Hawk. You'll learn a lot and it may even convince you that Christianity isn't so bad."

Hawk smiled, "Thanks for the invitation, Eagle, but I'm going to go visit my parents and family. Maybe I'll meet this Jesus there."

President Place shook their hands and watched them leave her office. When they were gone and the door safely closed, Roberta allowed herself to relax a bit.

Director Aires noticed as her shoulders slumped slightly and he even guessed what was on her mind.

He said, "Madam President, we'll put a guard on them, discreetly of course, but there'll be one, nonetheless. We've also doubled your son's protection, and we've more than doubled your own. We both know that this Committee will come at you with both barrels blazing in order to stop your re-election, but we'll be ready for them!

He opened his brief case, pulled out some papers and laid them on her desk.

"Let me go over these plans with you and get your final itinerary nailed down. You have a busy month ahead."

Roberta, shook off her gloom and began her plans for the final stage of her hopefully victorious election campaign.

*   *   *

On televisions all across America, a "Special News Bulletin" flashed onto the screen. Next, the beautiful and smiling face of Marla Brinkle filled their screens, "Good evening and welcome to this news update on Vice President Huggens. A surprise, "behind closed doors", agreement was reached today between Huggens's lawyers and the State Department. Huggens has pled guilty today to conspiracy to commit murder, kidnapping and treason in exchange for a protective custody life sentence. He'll cooperate fully with the authorities' investigation into a group calling themselves the Committee. The Committee is headed by Dr. Wilbur Kamerman and his man, Starvas Creen, both of whom are wanted for treason, the abduction and attempted murder of President Roberta Place and the abduction and assassination of Police Officer Joshua White."

Behind Marla, pictures of the two wanted men were flashed across the screen.

She wiped a tear from her eye, one of many she'd cried over Joshua's death, and continued, "If anyone sees these men or can help locate them, please, call the CIA at 1-800-HELP-CIA. There's a $10,000 reward for information leading to their capture. Under no circumstances should you try to apprehend them yourselves; they're considered armed and dangerous! Just call!

"On a happier note, I've arranged for my fiancée, Police Chief Grady O'Leary to be brought to the studio. He's secluded in the sound proof booth and can't hear us. He doesn't know it, but we're about to be married on National TV!"

Marla waved to the side and smiled as President Place and Senator Thomas Holstrum came out. Rev. Smith and Fr. Jerry Powell followed them.

Marla continued, "Father Powell, who incidentally was reinstated by the Catholic Church after Joshua's brutal murder, has agreed to marry us in the Catholic Church. I've secretly finished my instructions and have been baptized. If everyone would just step over to the chapel, we've set up..."

With that she walked over to a small but beautiful chapel complete with organ and flowers.

Marla turned to the home audience and said, "Grady's been trying to get me to talk about a date to get married, but I've been stalling until today! We'll be married tonight and have two days free time together, but we'll have to postpone our honeymoon until after next month's election. There's just too much to do between now and then and this was the only evening that we have enough airtime open to broadcast this. President Roberta Place has agreed to be my maid of honor, and she's brought her new running mate, Senator Thomas Holstrum, so all of you can get a good look at him before next month's election! A good-looker isn't he?"

Everyone laughed as Holstrum blushed, but he smiled good-naturedly through it all. Then they brought Grady O'Leary out. In the mean time Marla, had ducked behind a false wall and had put on a white wedding dress and veil. She stood off stage on one side and Grady on the opposite. Grady had that stunned, "deer caught in the head lights" look, but it didn't take him long to piece it together. He saw Marla first and then President Place, Fr. Powell, Rev. Smith and the Chapel. If that didn't give it away, the organ music did. When Marla started across stage; so did Grady. He was wearing his dress uniform and looked very impressive, the only thing brighter than his red hair was his perfectly white smile. After they met, they walked together to the chapel where Fr. Powell was waiting to join them in Holy Matrimony.

"We are gathered here today to join..."

*   *   *

Starvas Creen pulled out his gun and shot the television screen.

Dr. Kammerman, who'd, been in a deep sleep,

251

jumped up and fell out of bed, yelling, "What's happening? Did they find us?"

Creen looked down at the doctor with disgust and for a fleeting moment thought of plugging him right then, but he thought, with some disappointment, *"No! I need his connections, for now anyway."*

Creen put the gun away and said, "It was disgusting doctor. That Chief O'Leary and that reporter woman, Marla Brinkle was getting married on live television. They barely mentioned us except to plaster our faces across every T.V. screen in America. They've ruined us and made it very hard to get around now that everyone knows our faces."

He slumped onto his own bed, thought deeply for a moment, and a smile crossed his face.

Creen said, "Hey Doc, it just occurred to me, they're going to wait a month or so to go on their honeymoon. You know after the election? So this month, I'll work on punishing the President for her part in this and then I'll come up with something extra special for the newly wed couple! They'll wish they'd never crossed swords with me! I'll make sure of it!"

Both men smiled as their mad evil plans began to form in their black hearts.

*   *   *

Jesus Christ stood, from where He sat at His Father's right hand, and said, "My friends, We've asked you to gather here so We can thank you for all of your hard work and holy prayers. Satan's been getting bolder and bolder as the years have moved on, and he's about to push his boldest plan to date! He's raging through the earth trying to devour every human soul in sight. For you, the danger is over but the battle is not! You've each fulfilled your duties beyond My fondest desires and for that We're eternally grateful..."

As Jesus talked, Joshua White and Patricia White stood with their arms around each other's waist as tears of joy run down their cheeks. Joshua had never been happier...Ever! His first week in heaven had been spent celebrating with old and new friends, with family and then there was his reunion with Patricia. He'd known that heaven would be a nice place, a wonderful place, but nothing had prepared him for the feelings of well being, wonder and the glory of God's constant presence!

Joshua smiled as he looked around and he thought as he waved to Moses, who smiled and waved back, *"Never did I think that I'd one day stand shoulder to shoulder with Abraham, Moses, Peter and Paul, yet here they are! Praise be to the God of the living!"*

Jesus had stopped talking and suddenly Joshua realized that while he'd been daydreaming, Jesus had mentioned his name and everyone was suddenly watching him.

Patricia nudged him and he finally had to say, "I'm sorry, Lord, but I'm afraid I'm still in awe of the presence of all of these great saints and Yourself! What did you say?"

Everyone laughed and Jesus said, "I simply reminded everyone of your wonderful accomplishments while you lived on earth and I asked you to step up here with me if you would please."

Josh just stood there stunned for a moment and

then slowly approached the front of the ranks of saints and angels that surrounded the Lord in a huge circle. As Josh neared the spot where the Lord stood, he was surprised that God's presence was no more or less present here than He was in the back of the ranks. "*He seems to be equally present to all in heaven, just as he is to those on earth,*" Josh thought as he grabbed Jesus' extended hand and then embraced him in love.

Jesus turned to the multitude of heavenly hosts, both human and angelic, "We're granting Joshua White a special privilege. One that hasn't been granted to any human, other than Myself, since Moses and Abraham visited Me on the mountain top all those many years ago. We're allowing Joshua to stay directly involved in some specific aspects of the spiritual war that Satan is currently waging on earth. During this next stage of the battle when the Committee tries to take control of the world, Joshua's help will be crucial and that's why he's needed here rather than on earth."

Jesus turned to Joshua and said with a smile, "We always seem to be calling you to bigger and greater things, Joshua, and you can freely refuse, but hear Me out before you decide either way."

"As a human on earth, you did an outstanding job of teaching others about their spiritual lives and responsibilities and We blessed your work with many miracles and signs. Now, however, you're free from earthly bonds, weaknesses and dangers. You're now a little closer to the angels in your power and, with the special permission of my Father, you're to be allowed to return to earth with Aaron as your guide and you'll be allowed to serve in Aaron's army at least for this next phase of the battle.

"Josh, you must understand that this is an honor and a privilege. It's not that we don't think that Aaron can do it without you but your skill and experience will be helpful. Besides, my Father and I, along with all the angels concerned with this project, agree that you've earned the right to fight, if prematurely, in my heavenly army. What do you say? Interested?"

Josh bowed to one knee, tears of joy still running down his face, as he bowed his head to the ground and said, "Of course I accept and I only hope that I prove worthy of this great honor, my Lord!"

All around angels pulled their swords to their chests then raised them in respect of this warrior, who'd already proven himself in battle. They yelled in one glorious voice, "Holy and Great is our God's wisdom!"

Worl, the great Captain of the Angelic Guard, nodded his approval and turned from the joyful scene. His ever-present guards, Right and Left, rose with him in perfect unison and they turned toward earth yet again.

Worl thought as they passed through the veils that separate the two worlds, *The battle will rage hotter than ever, but Satan will never see God's latest move coming!*

He said to his guards, "This is going to be wonderful! Satan won't know what hit him!"

His guards smiled knowingly at each other and nodded their agreement.

To obtain additional copies of this or other Covenant books:
Visit your local Christian book retailer

or

On the Internet:
www.covenant-ministries.com

or

Send your request to:
A&L Enterprises
1531 Hwy 151
Ava, IL 62907